FROM THE NANCY DREW FILES

THE CASE: From the art galleries to the chic cafés, Nancy sets out to draw a portrait of a killer.

CONTACT: Professor Ellen Mathieson's biography of a famous painter leads to a study in murder.

SUSPECTS: David Fieldston—*He's succeeded in becoming Professor Mathieson's research assistant . . . now that her first choice is dead.*

Phillipe Leduc—*Josephine Solo threatened to sue him for copying her painting style . . . a threat she never had a chance to carry out.*

Jean-Luc Censier—*Art dealer or con artist? Either way he may have found that business can be murder.*

COMPLICATIONS: Did Professor Mathieson's research assistant die because he knew too much? Nancy's determined to find the answers . . . in a case in which the truth could prove deadly!

Books in The Nancy Drew Files® Series

#1 SECRETS CAN KILL
#2 DEADLY INTENT
#3 MURDER ON ICE
#4 SMILE AND SAY MURDER
#5 HIT AND RUN HOLIDAY
#6 WHITE WATER TERROR
#7 DEADLY DOUBLES
#8 TWO POINTS TO MURDER
#9 FALSE MOVES
#10 BURIED SECRETS
#11 HEART OF DANGER
#12 FATAL RANSOM
#13 WINGS OF FEAR
#14 THIS SIDE OF EVIL
#15 TRIAL BY FIRE
#16 NEVER SAY DIE
#17 STAY TUNED FOR DANGER
#18 CIRCLE OF EVIL
#19 SISTERS IN CRIME
#20 VERY DEADLY YOURS
#21 RECIPE FOR MURDER
#22 FATAL ATTRACTION
#23 SINISTER PARADISE
#24 TILL DEATH DO US PART
#25 RICH AND DANGEROUS
#26 PLAYING WITH FIRE
#27 MOST LIKELY TO DIE
#28 THE BLACK WIDOW
#29 PURE POISON
#30 DEATH BY DESIGN
#31 TROUBLE IN TAHITI
#32 HIGH MARKS FOR MALICE
#33 DANGER IN DISGUISE
#34 VANISHING ACT
#35 BAD MEDICINE
#36 OVER THE EDGE
#37 LAST DANCE
#38 THE FINAL SCENE
#39 THE SUSPECT NEXT DOOR
#40 SHADOW OF A DOUBT
#41 SOMETHING TO HIDE
#42 THE WRONG CHEMISTRY
#43 FALSE IMPRESSIONS
#44 SCENT OF DANGER
#45 OUT OF BOUNDS
#46 WIN, PLACE OR DIE
#47 FLIRTING WITH DANGER
#48 A DATE WITH DECEPTION
#49 PORTRAIT IN CRIME
#50 DEEP SECRETS
#51 A MODEL CRIME
#52 DANGER FOR HIRE
#53 TRAIL OF LIES
#54 COLD AS ICE
#55 DON'T LOOK TWICE
#56 MAKE NO MISTAKE
#57 INTO THIN AIR
#58 HOT PURSUIT
#59 HIGH RISK
#60 POISON PEN
#61 SWEET REVENGE
#62 EASY MARKS
#63 MIXED SIGNALS
#64 THE WRONG TRACK
#65 FINAL NOTES
#66 TALL, DARK AND DEADLY
#67 NOBODY'S BUSINESS
#68 CROSSCURRENTS
#69 RUNNING SCARED
#70 CUTTING EDGE
#71 HOT TRACKS
#72 SWISS SECRETS
#73 RENDEZVOUS IN ROME
#74 GREEK ODYSSEY
#75 A TALENT FOR MURDER
#76 THE PERFECT PLOT
#77 DANGER ON PARADE
#78 UPDATE ON CRIME
#79 NO LAUGHING MATTER
#80 POWER OF SUGGESTION
#81 MAKING WAVES
#82 DANGEROUS RELATIONS
#83 DIAMOND DECEIT
#84 CHOOSING SIDES
#85 SEA OF SUSPICION
#86 LET'S TALK TERROR
#87 MOVING TARGET
#88 FALSE PRETENSES
#89 DESIGNS IN CRIME
#90 STAGE FRIGHT
#91 IF LOOKS COULD KILL
#92 MY DEADLY VALENTINE
#93 HOTLINE TO DANGER
#94 ILLUSIONS OF EVIL
#95 AN INSTINCT FOR TROUBLE
#96 THE RUNAWAY BRIDE
#97 SQUEEZE PLAY
#98 ISLAND OF SECRETS
#99 THE CHEATING HEART
#100 DANCE TILL YOU DIE
#101 THE PICTURE OF GUILT

The
NANCY DREW
Files™
101

THE PICTURE OF GUILT

CAROLYN KEENE

AN ARCHWAY PAPERBACK
Published by POCKET BOOKS
New York London Toronto Sydney Tokyo Singapore

AN ARCHWAY PAPERBACK *Original*

An Archway Paperback published by
POCKET BOOKS, a division of Simon & Schuster Inc.
1230 Avenue of the Americas, New York, NY 10020

Produced by Mega-Books of New York, Inc.

ISBN: 0-671-88192-2

First Archway Paperback printing November 1994

10 9 8 7 6 5 4 3 2 1

Cover art by Cliff Miller

Printed in the U.S.A.

IL 6+

THE PICTURE OF GUILT

Chapter One

"Hold it, Nancy—right next to those gorgeous plums. They're the exact shade of your coat!"

Nancy Drew brushed her reddish blond hair from her face. She and her friend, George Fayne, were getting a firsthand look at a Paris street market in action. A crowd of shoppers flowed slowly between the two rows of stands that lined the block. The tables were heaped high with colorful fruits and vegetables.

George had stopped a few feet before Nancy to aim her pocket camera. "I can't get everything in," she complained, taking a step back. Then she added, "Oh, *pardon,* monsieur," as she bumped into a middle-aged man whose straw shopping basket contained several zucchini, some purple onions, and a bushy head of lettuce.

"Take one picture of me and another of the veggies," Nancy suggested, laughing, "and save some film for that fish store we just passed. Did you see all those crabs and lobsters? And the other shellfish—I don't even know the names of most of them."

George pressed the shutter release, then moved over to Nancy's side. "Well, if you find out, don't ever serve them to me," she said with a shudder. "Some of them were really ugly. I wouldn't want to meet them in a bad dream, never mind on a plate!"

"Don't worry," Nancy said, patting her friend's shoulder. "Dad's taking us out to dinner tonight. We'll tell him we want a place that doesn't feature shellfish."

Nancy's father, attorney Carson Drew, had come to Paris to settle the estate of a client. His old friend, Robert Morland, who owned a big apartment in Paris, offered to let him use it during his stay. He invited Nancy to come with him and bring her two best friends. Nancy's other close friend, Bess Marvin, already had plans to spend Thanksgiving with an old friend, so reluctantly she turned down the invitation. George was delighted to accept. The two girls had arrived at Charles de Gaulle Airport that morning at seven-thirty French time, which was still the middle of the night in River Heights. After a short rest and some freshening up at their apartment, they set out to explore the neighborhood, which was east of the Place de la Bastille, while Nancy's father went to an appointment.

George peered doubtfully at the string shopping bag on Nancy's arm. "Plums, apples, oranges, lettuce—you're not buying much," she commented. "Don't you think we ought to find a supermarket and stock up for the next few days?"

"Don't be silly," Nancy replied with a grin. "In Paris, people shop practically every day. That way, their food is always superfresh. Let's pick up some cheeses, a couple of pâtés, and a baguette. On the way back, we can stop at that little coffee-roasting shop we noticed and buy some tea and coffee. Then tomorrow we'll toss to see who goes out to get fresh baked croissants for breakfast."

"You mean they don't deliver?" George joked. "I'm crushed!"

A few minutes later the girls had bought everything they needed. After stopping to admire a stand piled high with roses, they made their way through the crowd of shoppers to the main street and the five-story building where they would be living for the next couple of weeks. The building was in the form of a hollow rectangle, with a long, narrow courtyard paved with cobblestones down the center.

They entered the courtyard and were starting up the stairs, when Nancy noticed a woman of about thirty-five coming down the stairs toward them. Her dark brown hair was cut in a short, asymmetrical style, one side chin length and the other an inch or so shorter. She had set off her turquoise wool jacket with a bright yellow silk scarf, casually knotted at her neck.

"Hello," the woman said. "You must be Bob Morland's guests. He told me to look for you. I'm Ellen Mathieson. I live just above you."

After Nancy and George introduced themselves and shook hands with her, the woman continued, "I was planning to knock on your door. I'm an American college professor, teaching and directing an exchange program for American students here. I'm having an open house this evening for our students. Would you like to come by and meet them? If you're not too jet-lagged, that is."

"Thanks very much," Nancy said after a quick glance at George. "It sounds like fun."

"Great. Anytime after eight," the woman said. "I'm off to buy some supplies before the market closes for lunch. See you this evening."

By the time George, Nancy, and Carson got back from dinner at a lively neighborhood bistro, it was nearly nine o'clock. The door to the courtyard was locked every evening after eight, but Carson punched in the code on the keypad next to it. The lock clicked, and they entered the courtyard. Nancy heard a buzz of voices from Professor Mathieson's apartment. Carson had to look over some papers, so Nancy and George dropped off their coats, then went up one more flight and knocked on Professor Mathieson's door.

She opened the door. "Nancy, George," she said with a big smile. "I'm glad you could make it. Come in and meet the gang."

At the end of a short hallway was the dining room. The table had been pushed back against the wall to make more space. Professor Mathieson led Nancy and George to a little group standing near the table. "Everybody. These are my new neighbors, George Fayne and Nancy Drew," the professor said. "Meet Pamela and David Fieldston and Keith Astor."

Pamela and David both were about twenty, and they both had blond hair, roundish faces, and upturned noses. "You two are related, right?" Nancy said, as Professor Mathieson strolled away.

"We're twins," Pamela replied with a laugh.

"Fraternal of course," David added, smiling.

Keith, a tall guy in his midtwenties, had a powerful chest and slim waist, set off by black jeans, a black shirt buttoned to the neck, and a black leather vest. He brushed a lock of dark hair off his face and fixed an intense gaze on Nancy. "Why are you arriving so late in the semester?" he asked.

Nancy quickly explained that they were in

Paris for just a couple of weeks. Then she added, "But what about you? You're here for the whole year? Are you all studying French?"

"I am," Pamela replied. "But Keith is a painter and David is in art history. One great thing about our exchange program is that we can take courses in different subjects at different branches of the University of Paris."

"Art history? Paris must be the perfect place to study that," George remarked. "Just think of all the great artists who've worked here."

"That's true, George," David said. "And Professor Mathieson is very well known in the field. She's working on a biography of Josephine Solo, the American painter who died last spring here in Paris, where she lived most of her life. Professor Mathieson and Solo were good friends."

"Solo?" Nancy said. "I think I read something about her. She was kind of eccentric, wasn't she?"

Pamela giggled. "She certainly was! When she first came to Paris, she took her easel and paints outside every time it rained—"

"Which is pretty often," David interjected.

"Wearing a bright yellow rain suit and hip boots, the kind Maine lobstermen wear," Pamela continued. "After the first couple of times, everybody knew who she was."

"Her *Paris Rain* paintings are worth a fortune now," David declared. "Museums and collectors all over the world want them. They're in greater demand than her later work."

"For good reason, too," Keith told him. "Those hyperrealist canvases she did later, with every tiny detail perfect, were technically very good, but they didn't have any of the power of her earlier abstracts."

He gazed at Nancy and George again. "Come see for yourselves," he added. "There are a couple of good examples in the other room."

Nancy and George followed him into the living room, where a dozen or so students were scattered around, chatting. Keith indicated a painting on the wall over the small console piano. It was of a checker tablecloth, a cup of coffee, and a plate of cinnamon buns, done in such exacting detail that Nancy could almost smell the coffee. The only odd feature in the painting was a gaunt, bluish hand reaching for one of the pastries.

"The title is *Depast for the Reparted,*" David said from behind Nancy. "Solo was playing with the words *repast for the departed.* That's supposed to be the hand of a dead friend. Solo loved weird jokes."

"I think I'm going to have nightmares tonight," George commented.

"Now look at this abstract over here," Keith said, gesturing toward the fireplace.

At first all Nancy saw in the painting was a swirl of muted colors, mostly blues and grays.

Gradually, however, she began to sense wet streets and a brooding sky and, in the distance, the beckoning lighted windows of a friendly café.

"It's hard to believe that the same artist did both paintings," Nancy remarked. "Why did she change her style so totally?"

"Money and fame, if you ask me," Keith said. "Lots of painters were doing abstracts, though they weren't as good as hers, but she was one of the first to paint in that hyperrealist style, so she attracted a lot of publicity and made some significant sales. Not that I blame her. Artists have as much right to make money as insurance salesmen."

"Cynical as always," David said, with a hostile glance at Keith. Then he turned to Nancy and said, "You should ask Professor Mathieson that question. She probably knows more about Solo's life and work than anyone else in the world."

Pamela stared unhappily at Keith, then at her brother. "I hope you two aren't going to argue," she said. "This is a party, remember?" She turned to George and Nancy and added, "Come meet some of the others."

During the next hour Nancy and George chatted with a woman doctoral student from New York who was studying Paris street musicians, a girl from Oklahoma who had joined the program after a single semester of French and admitted that she was just beginning to understand what people said to her, and a tall, handsome dance major named James, who immediately offered George a personally guided tour of Paris.

While George was arranging to meet him the next evening, Nancy took in the rest of the crowd. The party had started to thin out. Both Keith and David had apparently left, but Pamela was in the other room, helping to clear the table. She noticed Nancy standing alone and came over.

"My favorite café is just down the street," she said. "Would you and George like to join me for a hot chocolate?"

"I'd like to," Nancy told her. "Let me check with George."

After thanking Professor Mathieson and saying good night to the others, the three girls went out and found a small table in the window of the café. Half a dozen people were standing at the nearby bar, sipping tiny cups of coffee. Outside, the street was crowded with pedestrians and cars. Pamela explained that, in addition to the Bastille Opera House only a short distance away, there were half a dozen movie theaters and music clubs in the neighborhood.

She broke off to wave to a dark-haired guy in a black leather jacket who was walking past with a briefcase under his arm. He looked around and waved back but didn't stop. He quickly joined the throng of people on the sidewalk.

"That was Jules Daubenton," Pamela told them. "He's Professor Mathieson's research assistant for her new book. I wonder what he's doing here at this hour? He lives over on the Left Bank. Maybe he got the time wrong for—"

Pamela broke off her sentence. From nearby came the squeal of brakes and the blare of a truck's horn. An instant later they heard screams of terror. Nancy jumped to her feet.

A man came running into the café, shouting. The man behind the bar reached for a telephone.

Pamela stood up and stepped over to the bar, where she spoke a few words to the first man. White faced, she quickly sat down again. "How horrible!" she exclaimed. "Somebody's been hit by a truck. A young guy in a leather jacket, he says." Eyes widening, she turned to George and Nancy. "You don't think . . . it couldn't be Jules, could it?"

Chapter Two

"Come on," Nancy said urgently. "Let's find out what happened." She hurried out of the café, with George and Pamela close behind. Halfway down the block, just across the street from Nancy's building, a crowd had gathered on the sidewalk, spilling out onto the street. Just beyond, a truck was stopped in the middle of the road, its door open and its lights blinking. From somewhere nearby came the two-toned horn of an emergency vehicle.

As the girls moved closer, edging through the growing crowd, a bright red emergency truck came speeding up, followed closely by a white ambulance and two dark blue police cars. The blue rotating lights on their roofs cast spooky flashes on the solemn faces of the onlookers.

Nancy was nearing the center of the crowd when she heard people start murmuring anxiously to one another. She made out one word, repeated over and over—*mort.* Dead! She peered over the shoulders of the people just in front of her. A uniformed first-aid official was kneeling next to a crumpled body in the street. He raised his head to another member of his team and shook it slowly.

Two gendarmes, or police officers, began urging the crowd back onto the sidewalk to make room around the accident victim.

Pamela gripped Nancy's arm tightly. "Oh!" she gasped. "It *is* Jules! How awful!"

Nancy put an arm around the stunned girl's shoulders. But even as she did so, her eyes were searching the street. Jules had been carrying a briefcase when he walked past the café, just minutes before. Where was it now? Had the first-aid squad or police recovered it? No, they were all empty-handed, and she didn't think there had been time to put it anywhere.

A thief? He would have to have been very quick and very cold-blooded to grab something from a dying man. Still, sharp, ruthless thieves did exist.

"Nancy?" George said in an undertone. "I don't see that poor guy's briefcase anywhere."

Nancy nodded grimly. "I was just thinking the same thing. We ought to ask a few questions."

Pamela swiveled her head between Nancy

and George, wide-eyed. "What are you talking about?"

Before Nancy could reply, she heard a portly man in a gray double-breasted suit saying, to no one in particular, "I was only steps away when it happened. I saw it all—all!"

Nancy turned to him. "Pardon me, monsieur," she said in French. "But I know the victim. Can you tell me what happened?"

"Yes, of course." The man pursed his lips, then said, "I noticed the victim at once because he had a strange gleam in his eye. He moved past me, very fast, into the street. A moment later I heard the truck's horn. When I turned to look, I saw that there was no hope. The front wheel had passed over him completely."

Nancy repressed a shudder. "Was anyone else nearby?"

The man shrugged. "But of course. The streets are crowded now, when the cinemas finish. But I am sure the driver was not at fault, and I will say the same to the police. If someone dashes into the street, right in front of you, what are you to do?"

A sharp-faced woman in a short black dress and red jacket turned and said, "You say he dashed? Bah! Another man, who was in too much of a hurry to look where he was going, knocked this poor man into the path of the truck. He didn't even stop to see what he had done."

"You mean you saw this happen?" George demanded. "You should tell the police, at once!"

"But I really saw nothing," she said, in a taut voice. "This is what people are saying, that's all."

Nancy was sure that the woman was lying, that she had seen the whole episode but was simply unwilling to get involved. The woman turned and slipped quickly into the crowd before Nancy could find out what the other man looked like or whether the woman had noticed Jules's briefcase.

As the medical squad lifted Jules's body into the ambulance, one of the police officers came over, notebook in hand. In French he asked, "Is there someone who saw what happened?"

The man in the double-breasted suit nodded and began repeating his story. Near the truck, another officer was questioning a white-faced man in blue coveralls and a cloth cap. The truck driver, almost certainly, Nancy decided. At this point, the ambulance pulled away, and the crowd slowly dispersed. Nancy knelt down to look under the nearby parked cars, but there wasn't any sign of Jules's briefcase.

"What are you searching for, mademoiselle?"

Nancy stood up. A third police officer was eyeing her warily.

"Excuse me, officer," she said. "I'm an American and I knew who the victim was. He had a briefcase with him tonight. Do you know what happened to it?"

"Your papers, please?" the officer replied. He took Nancy's passport and copied down her name, birthdate, and passport number, then asked for her address in Paris. "What can you tell me about this incident?" he asked, as he handed back her passport.

"Nothing, really," Nancy replied. "My friends and I were in a café down the street. We saw Jules—the victim—go by just before he was killed. He was carrying a briefcase, but now I don't see it anywhere."

The gendarme frowned. "We found no brief-case when we reached the scene," he said. "It is very regrettable, but even in Paris we have thieves. I assure you that if it is found, it will be returned to the victim's family. You and your friends did not see the accident, then?"

"No," Nancy replied. Pamela and George nod-ded their agreement.

"Very well. Thank you for your cooperation," the officer said. He touched his hand to his cap, then walked away.

Nancy turned her attention to Pamela. "Are you okay?" she asked.

Pamela nodded soberly. "I guess so. I've never seen anybody I know dead before. I can't get the picture of him out of my mind." She glanced across the street and added, "Look, Professor Mathieson's light is still on. Do you think we ought to tell her what happened?"

Nancy took a deep breath. "She'll have to hear it from someone," she said.

They crossed the street, entered the building, and climbed to Professor Mathieson's apartment. She opened the door on the first knock.

"Well, it certainly took you—" she began, then broke off as she recognized Nancy, George, and Pamela. "Oh, hi. Sorry, I was expecting someone else. Come on in."

As they filed in, she noticed their grim expressions. "What is it?" she asked. "Is something wrong?"

"I'm afraid so," Pamela replied, her voice quivering. "It's Jules. He was in an accident."

"Jules? But I spoke to him earlier. He was planning to see me tonight. Was it serious? Where is he?" In the tense silence that followed, Professor Mathieson's face blanched. "What is it? Surely you don't mean . . ."

Gently, Nancy explained what had happened. Professor Mathieson stared at her, unbelieving, before sinking onto the couch. Pamela sat down next to her and took her hand.

"I can't . . ." Professor Mathieson began, then stopped to clear her throat. "You never expect something like this to happen to someone you know. Now that I think of it, I did hear sirens, but I didn't think anything about it. I was in the kitchen, cleaning up. I didn't even go to the window to see . . ." She fell silent, burying her face in her hands.

Nancy waited a few moments before asking, "Do you think he was on his way here?"

Professor Mathieson raised her head and nodded. "I know he was. We get together three or four times a week to go over what he's doing and where we should go next. We were scheduled to meet tomorrow afternoon. But tonight he called and asked if he could come right over. He said he had made an amazing discovery. I asked him what, of course, but he said he wanted to explain it to me in person. I wonder what it was," she added in a faraway voice. "I suppose now I'll never know. Poor Jules!"

Nancy met George's eyes. She could tell that her friend shared her thoughts. Had the evidence for Jules's amazing discovery been in his briefcase? And had someone stolen it and pushed Jules under the truck to keep him from revealing his discovery?

"What specifically was Jules working on?" Nancy asked.

"He was helping me with my book about Josephine Solo," Professor Mathieson replied. "He was compiling an account of her day-to-day activities during the last year of her life. It's tedious work, but details are essential for a project like mine. And we're under very heavy deadline pressure."

She turned to Pamela and asked, "Do you think David would be willing to take over for Jules? I know he felt bad when I gave the position to Jules instead of him."

"Oh, he got over that a long time ago," Pamela

replied. "And I'm sure he'd be thrilled at the chance to work more closely with you, Professor. That reminds me, I've got to get home. David must be wondering what happened to me."

"Ask him to come by and see me tomorrow," Professor Mathieson said. "I know it sounds heartless of me, but I can't let my project lose momentum, even in the face of a tragedy."

The professor walked Pamela to the door. Nancy and George waited in the living room. When she returned, Nancy said, "Professor Mathieson, I should tell you that I've done a lot of detective work. And it seems to me that there may be more to this accident than meets the eye."

Professor Mathieson returned slowly to the sofa. "Of course," she said. "Bob Morland did say something to me about your talent as a detective. But are you sure you're not imagining a mystery where none exists? Traffic accidents happen every day."

"Maybe I am," Nancy admitted. "But there are some details about what happened to Jules that have aroused my suspicions." She explained about the missing briefcase, then told of the woman who thought someone had knocked Jules into the street.

Professor Mathieson stared at her. "You're suggesting that Jules was murdered!"

Nancy hesitated. "Not necessarily," she said.

"It could have been an ordinary mugging that went wrong."

"It's a pretty weird coincidence, though," George pointed out. "Jules is hurrying over here with what he calls an amazing discovery, and a thief just happens to steal his briefcase?"

Professor Mathieson nodded slowly. "I see your point."

"What was this discovery of his? Do you know?" Nancy asked.

"Not at all," Professor Mathieson replied. "He didn't give me any hint. All he said was that he couldn't expect me to believe it unless I had the evidence right in front of me."

"Then he *did* have the evidence in that briefcase!" George exclaimed.

Professor Mathieson reacted with surprise. "Why, yes, I suppose he must have. Oh, dear—it's beginning to look as if there may be something to your suspicions, after all."

"You said earlier that Jules and David were rivals," Nancy said. "Is there any—"

"No, no!" Professor Mathieson said, cutting her off. "*Rivals* is too strong a word. They were both candidates for the same position, that's all. David is a fine student, very well qualified, but in the end I decided that Jules's native command of French made him the better choice for the job."

"But I thought you just taught American exchange students," Nancy commented.

"I teach one class outside of the exchange program, and that's how I got to know Jules."

"Was David upset and angry about not being chosen for the job?" George asked.

"Upset, naturally," the professor replied. "But more disappointed than angry."

Nancy thought that as of the next day David would have the research post he so badly wanted. Did he want it badly enough to steal important documents from his rival? That seemed pretty farfetched. Anyway, how could he have known that Jules was on his way to see Professor Mathieson with important documents in his briefcase?

"You said that Jules called to ask if he could come by," Nancy said to Professor Mathieson. "When was that? Was anyone here at the time?"

The professor frowned as she concentrated. "I'm sorry. All I can tell you is that it was near the end of the party," she said. "There were a number of people still here, but I have no idea who."

"Professor Mathieson," George asked. "Did you tell anybody that Jules was on his way here? Also, why wasn't he at the party? Didn't you invite him?"

"Of course. And, please, call me Ellen." She paused to collect her thoughts. "Jules came to the first of our open houses, back in September, but I think he felt a bit out of place. Everyone but he was American. As for mentioning that he was coming by this evening, I don't recall doing so. I might have, but I doubt it."

This seemed to be a blind alley. Nancy decided to try a different route. "Ellen, it sounds as if you kept close tabs on Jules's work. Can you remember what, specifically, he was working on the past few days?"

"Yes, of course," Ellen replied. "As I said earlier, he was researching Josephine's last days, finding out who she met, where she went, what she did. It wasn't an easy job. I was a close friend of Josephine, you know, perhaps her closest friend in recent years, but even with me she could be almost pathologically secretive."

She paused, then added, "Life is full of strange ironies, isn't it? That Jules should spend his last days investigating Josephine's last days, then die under the wheels of a truck."

Nancy was puzzled. "It is sad," she said, "but why do you call it ironic?"

"Didn't you know?" Professor Mathieson asked. "Josephine Solo died in a traffic accident last spring. She was killed instantly when she fell in front of a truck only a few blocks from here."

Chapter Three

NANCY GASPED slightly at Ellen's revelation. She noticed George, who was staring at Ellen in shock.

"Josephine Solo was killed in exactly the same way as Jules?" George exclaimed. "What a coincidence!"

"Yes," Ellen said slowly. "I suppose it is."

"You sound doubtful," Nancy remarked. "Why? Was there something suspicious about her death?"

The professor studied her clasped hands. "Not really," she replied in a far-off voice. "Accidents do happen every day. It's just—well, Jo's death has always puzzled me. She was usually such a careful person, the kind who checks both ways before crossing the street, even if she has the right of way. All I can think is that she had something on her mind, something that distracted her at the critical moment. I was hoping that Jules's research would help uncover what it might have been."

"I know Josephine Solo was very well known as an artist," Nancy said. "Was she rich, too?"

Ellen laughed. "She lived very comfortably from the sales of her paintings, but she was no millionaire. If she had left some completed canvases, they would be worth quite a lot now. But Jo's productivity must have dropped off a lot. After her death, we found only one finished painting in her studio."

"Really? Did that surprise you?" asked George.

Ellen rolled her eyes. "To say the least! You see, Jo left her entire estate to me. We had an understanding that I would sell a few of the canvases and use the money to endow a Josephine Solo room to house the others in my university's art museum back in the States."

She glanced at the painting over the mantel for a moment, then added, "It's such a shame that it didn't work out that way. But Jo must have expected to have many more productive years. How could she know she would die relatively young? She was only in her fifties, you know."

Nancy said, "Could somebody have stolen paintings from her studio after she died?"

"What an astonishing idea," Ellen exclaimed. "I wonder—but, no, it's not possible. I flew over the same day that I heard the news, and the police turned over her keys to me after her lawyer explained that I was her executor. And to be honest, it was pretty clear from her studio that she hadn't been working in several months.

"You poor dears," Ellen added, glancing at her watch, then getting to her feet. "Your jet lag will be catching up with you soon. Luckily, you don't have far to go before you sleep."

As Nancy stood up, she realized how tired she was. But she found a last reserve of energy. "I'd like to know more about Solo's last months," she said. "Can we talk tomorrow morning?"

Ellen shook her head. "I'm afraid not. I have a class tomorrow at ten. But if you like, I'll let you check over some of Jo's papers. French universities are notoriously short on space, so I'm using the back bedroom as an office. Can you be here by nine or nine-fifteen?"

"We'll be here," Nancy replied, then struggled to hold back a powerful yawn. Ellen walked the girls to the door and let them out. After saying good night to Ellen, Nancy and George went downstairs to their apartment.

In the living room Carson was seated near the fireplace with a stack of papers on his lap. He greeted them when they came in and took off his reading glasses. "Well, have you two been having fun, taking in all the sights?" he asked.

"Not exactly," Nancy replied. She recounted

the evening's events, including the party at Ellen Mathieson's, Jules's death, and their discussion afterward with Ellen.

As she spoke, Carson nibbled thoughtfully on an earpiece of his reading glasses. When she finished, he asked, "I take it you sense a mystery in all this?"

"More than one," Nancy replied eagerly. "The most obvious is the missing briefcase. Who took it, and why? And what about the fact that Jules and Solo died in such similar ways? Could they both have been murdered, and by the same person?"

Carson raised one eyebrow questioningly. "What makes you think that?" he asked.

"It's just too much of a coincidence," Nancy replied. "According to Professor Mathieson, Solo was a very careful person, not the kind who would wander out in front of a truck. And there's at least one witness who says that somebody knocked Jules into the street."

"A vanished witness," Carson pointed out. "Not very helpful."

"True," Nancy admitted. "But we do know that Jules was doing research on Solo's last months. It's a reasonable hypothesis that his death is somehow related to something he discovered. What if he found evidence that pointed to her killer? Or what if Solo's killer *thought* that Jules had uncovered such evidence?"

"That's quite a string of ifs," Carson replied.

"But what if we get the evidence to prove we're right?" asked George.

"That's a different matter," Carson said. "But let me just mention that, if you are right, and if this hypothetical killer finds out that you're checking into the deaths of Solo and Jules, you girls could be in danger, too. I know you both too well to suggest that you drop the investigation, but please be careful."

"We will, Dad," Nancy said, but another big yawn muffled her words.

"Okay, that's it," Carson said with a laugh. "Off to bed, you two! The case will have to wait until tomorrow morning."

Promptly at nine the next morning, Nancy and George rang Ellen's bell. She opened the door at once. This morning, she was wearing a dark blue dress with a wide, bright red belt that matched her shoes. Her face was tired and drawn.

"Come in, girls," she said. "I just made a fresh pot of coffee, if you'd like some. I didn't get much sleep last night, thinking about poor Jules. Do you really believe that the work he was doing for me led to his death?"

The most honest answer would have been "Yes," but Nancy diplomatically said, "I think we have to check out that possibility."

Ellen nodded. "Yes, I can understand that.

Now, you said you were interested in Jo's last few months, right?"

"That's right," Nancy said.

"Very well," Ellen said with a grave smile. She led them into the living room and pointed to a small desk in one corner. "What I've done is to pull out photocopies of Jo's datebook and address book for last year and the first two months of this year. There's also a file of letters Jo received during that period."

"Terrific," George said.

"I'd rather these materials didn't leave the apartment," Ellen continued. "Would you mind using them here? When you're done, just pull the door shut behind you. It locks automatically."

"This is really helpful of you," Nancy said. "I hope we're not putting you to all this trouble for nothing."

"Frankly, I hope you *are,*" Ellen replied. "I would find it almost a comfort to be able to think that the deaths of my old friend and my research assistant were simply cruel accidents. The alternative is much more terrifying. Oops—I'd better run or I'll be late for class."

She grabbed a plastic portfolio from the desk and hurried out the door.

As the door closed, Nancy looked over at George. "Why don't you start reading through that file of letters?" she asked. "I want to make a list of people Solo was in touch with during those last months. Then we'll see if we can manage to talk to any of them."

"Sure, Nan," George said. She took the thick file over to the sofa and got to work on it.

Nancy found a pad and pen and opened Solo's appointment book. After the first page, she realized it was going to be hard work. Like a lot of people, Solo had simply jotted enough information in her datebook to remind her of her engagements. An entry such as *kr 4 dm* must have meant something to her, but for someone else to decipher would be difficult, if not impossible.

As a first step Nancy copied all the entries onto her pad, in a long column. Then she studied the result. Most of the entries were one or two letters, followed usually by a number, and sometimes by more letters. Nancy chewed on the end of her ballpoint pen and stared into space.

What was the most important information to remember about an appointment? Obviously, *who, when,* and *where,* in more or less that order. In that case the numbers probably stood for the time Solo was to meet somebody, and the first set of letters was probably the person's initials. The other letters? An abbreviation for the name of the place they had agreed to meet?

To test this theory, she turned to the address book. It was almost impossible to read, filled with names, scratched out and overwritten addresses and telephone numbers, and cryptic notes. Still, in half an hour of cross checking, she managed to track down names that fit most of the initials. But who on earth was BW? Solo had met him or her a lot during the last few months of her life, but there was no trace of anyone with those initials in the address book.

The places, if that really was what they were, turned out to be even harder. Then Nancy had a flash of inspiration. Solo was a painter. What would be more natural than for her to meet people at a museum? Nancy scanned the list again, while trying to recall the names of the important museums of Paris. *LOU* was obviously the Louvre, which meant that *ORS* was probably the Orsay Museum, the second most important museum in Paris. But what could *DM* stand for?

In a nearby bookcase, Nancy found a guidebook to Paris and scanned the list of museums for one that started with *D.* There didn't seem to be any. She returned to Solo's address book. No one on the *M* page had a first name that began with *D.* With a feeling of futility, Nancy turned to the *D* page and began to scan it.

Suddenly she snapped her fingers. There it was, halfway down the page: Deux Magots, the famous Left Bank café, a favorite meeting place of artists, writers, and intellectuals since the early twentieth century. Mystery solved.

"Nancy!" George suddenly said. "Look what I just found."

She passed over a letter written on the stationery of an art gallery on the Left Bank. Nancy read:

> My dear Jo—
>
> After so many years of such close association, it gives me much pain to learn that you are saying lies about me and the way I lead my business. This must not continue. If you will not learn to hold your tongue, you will oblige me to take measures—*strong* measures—to ensure that you slander no one ever again.

Chapter Four

NANCY READ through the note George had found once more, this time out loud. Then she met her friend's gaze.

"That's pretty obviously meant as a threat," she said. "What it amounts to is, 'Shut your mouth, or I'll shut it for good.'"

"And it's dated late February, not long before Solo was killed," George pointed out.

The note was signed Jean-Luc, in spidery handwriting. At the top of the page, under the name and address of the gallery, in small type was printed Jean-Luc Censier, Director. "I think Mr. Censier just moved to the top of our list of people to talk to." Nancy said. "I've got the names and addresses of four or five others who were in frequent touch with Solo before her death, too. After we talk to Censier, we should see how many of them we can track down."

"Do you think we're dressed well enough to go interviewing people?" George asked, indicating her turquoise turtleneck and black jeans.

Nancy, who was also wearing black jeans with an off-white Irish sweater, laughed. "Half the people I've seen on the street are wearing jeans," she said. "Jeans and leather jackets. Good thing we brought ours—they're just right for fall weather here."

They collected their notes and piled Ellen's materials neatly on the table. They left her apartment, closing the door carefully behind them. They stopped downstairs for their jackets before walking to the nearest station on the Paris métro, or subway. It was just a short walk in the direction of the Bastille. The sky was brilliant, dotted with fluffy clouds. Over the rooftops at the far end of the street, Nancy could see, gleaming in the sunlight, the gilded statue atop the column in the center of the Place de la Bastille. As they walked past the coffee-roaster's shop, she took a deep breath and let it out as a sigh of pleasure.

"I think I'm in love," George announced. "With Paris!"

Nancy grinned at her. Words didn't seem necessary.

The entrance to the métro was a green cast-iron structure in the form of twining branches and leaves, with tall lamps shaped like tulips at the corners. Downstairs, the girls bought a supply of tickets and passed through the turnstile, then studied the big wall map of the métro system.

"All those tangled colored lines look like my grandmother's knitting basket after the kitten got through with it," George said with a giggle.

Nancy located a métro stop near Censier's gallery, then traced it backward with her fingertip. "There we go—we only have to change trains once. Come on."

Less than half an hour later, Nancy and George were riding an escalator back to street level. On the other side of a wide, traffic-packed boulevard was a squat, squarish church whose stone walls were scarred by the centuries. Across from it was a crowded café whose many tables were screened from strollers by neatly trimmed hedges. The sign over the door read Aux Deux Magots.

"See that café? That was one of Solo's favorite places to meet people," Nancy said excitedly. "I'm starting to feel as if we're getting closer to her. And look, that's the rue Bonaparte. The gallery must be down that way."

The girls crossed the boulevard and walked past the church into a narrow street. Every other shop seemed to be an art gallery. The one they wanted had discreet gold lettering on the window. The door was locked. Nancy pressed the bell. A moment later the door opened with a click.

Nancy and George went in. As they were

scanning the smooth white walls hung with many canvases, a young woman in what looked like a genuine sixties white minidress came out of the back. "May I help you?" she asked in French.

"We'd like to speak to Monsieur Censier," Nancy replied.

"I'm sorry," the woman said. "He is away for the moment. He should be back in an hour, if you would like to return."

"Thanks, we'll do that," Nancy said.

As she stepped onto the sidewalk, someone almost bumped into her. She glanced up and recognized Keith Astor, the art student they had met the evening before at Ellen's open house.

"Hey, I know you," he said. "Nancy, right? And—"

"George."

Keith nodded at George's reply, without taking his eyes from Nancy's. Was he coming on to her, Nancy wondered, or was he simply one of those guys who couldn't help flirting with everyone?

"Sure, George," he said. "How are you guys doing? Checking out the Paris art scene?"

"Sort of," Nancy replied. "How about you?"

"Oh, hey, this is my turf," he said. "I'm taking classes at the École des Beaux-Arts, just down there, near the river. It's a little stodgy, but it's still one of the best art schools in the world. I'm on my way to lunch. Want to join me?"

Nancy hesitated. She and George had lots of work to do. On the other hand, Keith could be a valuable source of information about Jules and his friends—and enemies.

"Don't worry," Keith added. "For Paris, the place I'm going is super cheap. That's why all the kids from the Beaux-Arts hang out there."

He stepped off the curb, then jumped back as a noisy motorbike came zipping around the corner, narrowly missing him. Nancy, afraid that he might lose his balance, grabbed his shoulder.

"Those mobylettes!" he said angrily. "You have to watch yourself in this town. The people who ride them never pay attention to anyone!"

Nancy and George followed Keith a couple of blocks to a corner restaurant with checkered café curtains in the lower part of the wide windows. As they made their way through the crowded front room, at least half a dozen people waved or called out to Keith, who waved back.

The back room, like the front, was furnished with long wooden tables and benches. The tables were so crowded that Nancy didn't see any place for the three of them to sit. At one table a guy with a black beard was talking intently to a girl with bangs that came down past her eyebrows. Keith tapped the bearded guy on the shoulder, motioning for him to move over. The guy and his companion slid down, making room for three.

"There's a fixed menu," Keith explained, indicating a blackboard on the wall. "Appetizer, main dish, cheese, and dessert. Do you like salmon steak? That's the main dish today."

"Sounds terrific," George said as a waiter appeared with a basket of bread and three plates of ham, salami, hard sausage, and tiny pickles.

Nancy waited until Keith finished his first bite, then asked, "Did you hear about Jules?"

Keith's face grew sober. "Yes. One of the guys in the program called me this morning and told me," he replied. "How awful! People get killed in traffic accidents every day, but you never expect it to happen to someone you know."

"He was working for Professor Mathieson, wasn't he?" George asked.

"That's right," Keith said.

"I heard that David was pretty upset when Jules got that job," Nancy remarked. "Apparently he thought he should have gotten it instead."

Keith let his fork clatter to his plate. "A lot of people are too snoopy for their own good," he said, scowling. "Maybe they should try doing something worthwhile, instead of butting into other people's business."

Apparently feeling he had been a little too rude, he added, "Have you seen much of Paris so far? You can spend years in this town without seeing everything worthwhile."

The salmon steak was delicious, but Nancy felt too frustrated to enjoy it. Every time she or George asked Keith about people in the exchange program, he started talking about the attractions of Paris. He obviously knew the city really well—surprisingly well for someone who had only been there since September.

"You must have spent time in Paris before this year," Nancy remarked, after he gave them a list of four or five museums they shouldn't miss.

"So?" he replied flippantly. "Oh, did I mention the Cluny Museum? It's just a few blocks from here. The medieval tapestries are among the most famous in the world."

Nancy listened with interest, but she kept wondering why Keith was stonewalling. What was he afraid of giving away?

As they were starting their dessert of apple tart, a cute guy in jeans and a leather jacket stopped at the table.

"Keith," he said in accented English. "I was hoping I'd see you. There's a party Saturday night, at Didier's studio. You must come."

He glanced at George and Nancy and added, "Hello, I'm Alain. It will be much fun if you come, too. Here, I write you the address."

He scribbled something on a card and handed it to George, then walked away, giving them a casual wave.

"You're in luck," Keith said. "Alain and Didier give great parties. Listen, I've got to run. Maybe I'll see you on Saturday."

He stood up, put some money on the table and walked out, leaving his apple tart untouched.

"Well!" George said after he was gone. "I wonder what got to him?"

"I don't know," Nancy replied. "He certainly seemed to be hiding something, but what—"

She broke off her sentence. Through the open doorway into the front room, Nancy could just see out the front window. She stood to see better when she noticed Keith talking to someone beside him. She caught only a glimpse of his companion's face, but it was enough to recognize Pamela Fieldston and identify her starry-eyed expression. Pamela was apparently in the grip of a powerful crush.

"I think I found out one of the things that Keith was hiding," Nancy said, and told George what she had seen after she sat down.

"Pamela and Keith?" George mused. "Hmm—I didn't see anything between them at the party last night. I did notice that Keith and Pamela's brother didn't get along very well, though.

Nancy shrugged. "Yes, I did, too. Well, come on, let's see if Censier is back yet."

They paid the check and walked back to the gallery. Inside, the girl in the minidress was talking to a man in a fitted mouse-gray suit. His thick blue-gray hair formed three precise waves as it crossed his head, and his cheeks were freshly shaved and powdered.

"I am Jean-Luc Censier," he said as he crossed the room toward Nancy and George. From his expression, it was obvious that he had already decided they were wasting his time. "You wish to see me?"

"That's right," Nancy said, improvising quickly. "I'm an American college student doing a term paper on the artist Josephine Solo. I understand you knew her."

"Knew her?" Censier said with a sniff. "My dear girl, I was her exclusive dealer for over fifteen years. It was on my advice that she gave up her early style to develop the one that made her name world famous."

He waved a well-manicured hand toward a painting on the far wall. Nancy had already noticed it. In incredibly sharp detail, it showed a little girl lying on her stomach in tall grass, her chin cupped in her hands, seemingly unaware of the snake slithering across her ankle.

"Why would anybody want that hanging on their wall?" George demanded with a shudder.

"Last week a Japanese banker offered to buy it for more than the price of a very expensive sports car," Censier replied coldly. "The collector who put it on the market turned him down. So few paintings by Josephine Solo are on the market that their value is bound to increase dramatically in the next few years."

"Why are there so few?" Nancy asked.

"Solo took great pains with her work," the gallery owner replied. "Every small detail had to be exactly done. She never passed a painting on to me until she was absolutely satisfied with it. And sometimes, if that moment never arrived, she would destroy it. Some very good paintings ended up in her fireplace, alas."

"Was Josephine Solo a difficult person to work with?" Nancy asked. "I heard a rumor that toward the end of her life, you and she weren't on very good terms."

Censier narrowed his eyes at Nancy. "I thought as much," he said. "You are working for that American professor, are you not? When I refused to talk to the other person she sent, she decided to use your fresh young faces to charm me. Well, please tell her that it did not work."

Nancy felt a wave of irritation at herself. Had she really been that obvious? "I'm not sure I understand," she fumbled. "What other person?"

Censier's face turned red. Clenching his fists, he took a step toward her. "You know who I mean," he said through tight lips. "Daubenton, he called himself. And if you do not get out of here at once, I will see that you receive the same treatment he did!"

Chapter Five

HIS FACE FULL OF MENACE, the gallery owner took another step toward Nancy and George, but Nancy refused to back down. Straightening her shoulders, she told him in a quiet but firm voice, "I'd be careful what I say, if I were you. Do you realize that Jules Daubenton was killed less than twenty-four hours ago? Is that the treatment you're threatening us with?"

"What?" Censier pulled his head back in surprise. "If this is a joke, I find it in very bad taste."

"It's no joke," George quickly assured him. "Jules Daubenton was killed last night, hit by a truck. We saw it happen—well, practically."

Censier was silent for a moment. "I am very sorry, of course," he went on. "Even if I did not appreciate that young man's impolite questions and insulting insinuations."

"Questions and insinuations about your relationship with Josephine Solo?" Nancy asked.

When she saw the cords in the man's neck stand out, Nancy got ready to face another burst of temper from him, but it didn't come. Instead, he took a deep breath and said, "Josephine Solo was never easy to deal with. Anyone who knew her will tell you that. And toward the end of her life, she came to hold the most outrageous suspicions about people who had only her best interests at heart. We all forgave her, of course, but in my case, I felt that I had no choice but to end our business relationship. But it is still a very sensitive topic for me. There—I have nothing to add to that. If you will excuse me . . ."

As he started to turn away, George demanded, "What did you mean when you said we'd get the same treatment as Jules?"

"What?" He hesitated for a moment, then said, "He refused to leave when I asked. I had to tell him that I would call the police and have him arrested. Now, please—I am a very busy man."

Nancy and George left the gallery. "Let's find some place to sit down and share our reactions," Nancy said as they strolled down the sidewalk.

They walked back toward the métro and stopped at a sidewalk café in the bright sunlight. A waiter in a white apron and black vest was at the table only moments after they sat down. Nancy ordered a café crème for herself and a tea with milk for George, and then, as an afterthought, she asked for two croissants as well. The waiter nodded and made a swipe at the marble tabletop with his napkin.

"Censier's hiding something," Nancy said as the waiter walked away. "That note we found couldn't have been anything but a threat."

"He seems to like making threats," George replied. "He threatened us, he threatened Solo, and he threatened Jules, too. But the important question is, does he do anything about his threats?"

Nancy thoughtfully stared out at the sunlit square, then leaned back to allow the waiter to put their croissants and beverages on the tiny table. She added a sugar cube to her coffee with cream, then took a sip before saying, "That's one question. Another is, what did Solo accuse him of that led to the threats? My hunch is that she thought he was embezzling money from her."

"That fits," George said excitedly. "And then he killed her to keep the truth from coming out and ruining him!"

"Whoa! It's a long way from making vague threats to killing somebody," Nancy pointed out. "Even if Solo did find out that Censier was cheating her, that doesn't mean he murdered her."

George nodded regretfully. "No, I guess not. But it is possible. And what if Jules found evidence that Censier had been swindling Solo and let Censier know it? Censier could have decided to silence Jules."

Nancy shook her head. "I don't know—it seems like a pretty flimsy motive to me. What if Censier did cheat Solo, and the facts came out now? It wouldn't help his reputation, but is that enough to turn him into a murderer?"

"Do you think Solo was getting a little dotty?" George asked. "Censier seemed to say that he wasn't the only one of Solo's friends to be having problems with her."

"*That* we can check out," Nancy replied, taking out the list of names she had compiled from Solo's datebook. "Let's find a phone and see if we can talk to any of these people."

The waiter directed them to a coin phone on the lower level of the café. Twenty minutes later Nancy brushed her hair back from her forehead with an ink-stained hand and ruefully perused the scattered notes on her memo pad.

"Three out of five," she said. "That's not too bad, I guess. So, our first appointment is with somebody named Roger Henderson, who runs an American bookstore near Notre Dame Cathedral."

They walked down to the Seine, then strolled along it past one open-air bookstall after another. George wanted to stop and rummage through a bin of antique postcards, but Nancy took her arm and dragged her away. They arrived at the bookstore as it was reopening after a long lunch break. Henderson, a tall man with thinning white hair and lots of laugh lines around his blue eyes, was wheeling out a table loaded with used paperbacks. Nancy introduced herself.

"I'm glad to see so much interest in Josephine," he said. "It's a little late to help her peace of mind, but her work deserves the recognition."

Nancy and George followed him inside the shop. The shelves of books reached all the way to the high ceiling and seemed to lean inward, as if they were about to tumble to the floor. Nancy could see dust motes in the air. George sneezed.

"Sorry," the bookdealer said, smiling. "It's all I can do to keep the place in some kind of order. Dusting it would take an army. Now, what can I tell you about Josephine? We were friends for twenty years, but I never knew from month to month if she was speaking to me."

"Did she pick a lot of fights with people?" asked George.

Henderson hesitated. "Not exactly—but she was always moody and touchy, especially about her work. I don't think she was ever really happy with it, especially in the last ten years or so, but if anyone said anything about it that sounded like a slight, she went off like a rocket."

"Censier, the gallery owner, told us that he pretty much made Solo's career. Is that a fair statement?" Nancy asked.

Henderson pursed his lips and made a little

popping sound. "Not exactly," he repeated. "Jean-Luc's the one who turned her toward that hyperrealist stuff, true. But if you look at where her paintings are now, it's the early abstracts that are in museum collections. Because they're better and more honest, if you ask me. And of course, late last year they had a huge blowup and Jo broke off with him totally."

"What was it about?" Nancy asked.

"I hate to repeat vague rumors," the book-dealer replied. "All I know for sure is that Jo thought Jean-Luc was using her work in some sort of scheme that she didn't approve of. When she confronted him, he denied it, which simply made her madder than ever. Jo hated liars. I can't tell you more than that."

Nancy and George continued to question him, but he had little to add. Finally Nancy thanked him and they left. As they rode the métro to their next appointment, Nancy wondered whether Censier had broken off relations with Solo, as he had claimed, or whether she had fired him, as Henderson had implied. Henderson's version sounded more likely. He had no reason to distort the truth. Censier, on the other hand, would obviously prefer to hide the fact that a prestigious artist like Solo had quit his gallery.

They arrived at their stop, left the train, and walked upstairs to the street.

"Madame de Reduane," George said doubtfully, studying Nancy's notes. "Are you sure this is the right place?"

Nancy looked up at the elaborately carved facade of the building and the uniformed, white-gloved doorman who was watching them curiously. "This is the address," she replied.

As she and George approached the entrance, the doorman saluted and said, "Mesdemoiselles Dey-rew et Fay-ne? The countess is expecting you."

"Countess?" George mouthed silently to Nancy. Nancy raised her eyebrows and gave a slight shrug.

Another man in uniform took them up three floors in an elevator that looked like a polished brass cage. As the elevator came to a halt, the mahogany doors facing it opened. A girl in a black uniform and frilly white apron curtsied and said, "This way, please."

Nancy and George followed her into a huge living room crowded with antiques. The tall windows faced onto the Seine. In the distance the Eiffel Tower stood out lacelike against the sky.

Nancy was imagining the Countess de Reduane to be middle-aged and frighteningly elegant. The woman who appeared in the doorway was no more than thirty-five and was wearing jeans and a T-shirt.

"Hello, Nancy, George," she said, in a perfect American accent. "Have a seat. Would you like a soda or anything?"

She smiled at their surprise and confusion. "My dad's American," she explained, "and I spent part of my childhood in Philadelphia before we moved to Paris. I'm really curious about your call. Why me?"

Nancy explained about finding her name in Josephine Solo's appointment book.

"Dear Aunt Jo," the countess said wistfully. "Her death was such a loss—to the art world, of course, but to me personally, too."

"She was your aunt, Countess?" George asked, puzzled.

"Oh, please, call me Cynthia," she replied with a smile. "And, no, we were only distantly related. But she was one of my mother's oldest friends. And when I got to know her again, after I started collecting her work, it seemed natural to call her what I had as a child. She liked it. She was quite lonely in many ways."

Nancy took in the beautiful room. Half a dozen paintings hung on the walls. Four were abstracts and the other two realistic. "Are these all Solos?" she asked.

"That's right," Cynthia replied. "I was very lucky to find so many from her early period, and to buy them before the prices started to climb. Now, of course, they would be out of reach for an individual collector like me."

As the conversation continued, Nancy gradually realized that Cynthia hadn't known Josephine Solo well as a person, only as an artist. She claimed to know nothing at all about Solo's relationship with Censier or about any enemies the painter might have had.

Back on the sidewalk, George said, "That was a big, fat zero."

"Not quite," Nancy replied. "It tells us that one of the people Solo saw the most of in the last months of her life hardly knew her at all. Let's see what we can learn from the last person on our list, Gail Fountain."

"The woman who wrote those French cookbooks?" George demanded. "Wow—we have two of her books at home. Terrific recipes, but very complicated."

Fountain lived in a rundown building near the center of Paris. Nancy and George trudged up four flights of uncarpeted stairs and knocked on her door. No answer. They tried again. Finally they started to leave.

At that moment a woman who was in her forties, wearing a tweed skirt and Irish sweater, came barging up the stairs. The string shopping bag on her arm overflowed with vegetables.

"You must be George and Nancy," she said breathlessly in accented English. "I'm Gail Fountain. I'm so sorry I'm late. When I walk into a food store, I go into a trance. Please come in."

She led them into a big, cheerful kitchen dominated by a cast-iron restaurant range, and they sat down around one end of a long, time-scarred oak table.

"It's interesting," Fountain said, after Nancy explained that they were researching the last year of Solo's life. "I must have been as close to Jo as anyone, but after your call, I realized that there was so much I didn't know about her, especially in the last year or two."

"Why was that?" asked George. "Were the two of you out of touch?"

The food writer shook her head. "Not at all. We lunched together at least once a week and spoke on the phone even more often. But Jo kept things to herself. It was as if she was afraid that sharing them with others might spoil them."

After a pause she added, "Here's an example. The last few months before she died, Jo seemed happier than I'd ever seen her. I commented on it more than once, but she just smiled mysteriously and changed the subject."

"What do you think it meant?" Nancy asked.

"I don't know," Fountain replied. "I did wonder if she had fallen in love, but if she had, I have no idea with whom, or why she would keep it secret from her friends."

"A romance?" George asked dubiously. She and Nancy were climbing the stairs from the métro station to the street shortly after their visit to Gail Fountain. "Wouldn't you think we'd have heard about it before now?"

"Not if Solo was as close-mouthed as people have indicated. She could have been keeping it to herself," Nancy replied. "And people of all ages do fall in love. I wonder if Ellen has any ideas about it."

They were just passing a bakery. The window was filled with pastries of every sort. George grabbed Nancy's arm and said, "Look at that fabulous raspberry tart! Let's get one for dessert tonight."

Nancy laughed. "You sound like Bess! But you're right, it does look delicious."

They bought the tart and continued toward the apartment. They were just a few steps away, crossing the mouth of a narrow side street, when a sudden noise alerted Nancy.

She jerked her head around. A motorbike, the kind Keith had called a mobylette, had just veered away from the curb and was rapidly picking up speed. She and George were directly in its path.

Chapter Six

NANCY GRABBED GEORGE by the shoulders and jumped out of the way of the speeding mobylette. Her heel caught on one of the paving stones, but she managed to keep her balance and get a good look at the motorbike. The rider was wearing a full helmet with dark visor and a dark green jumpsuit—not much hope of identifying him or her from that. But fastened to the luggage carrier of the motorbike was a large metal box with the words Pizza Pow! in bright red.

"These *motards,*" a middle-aged man said angrily in French. "Never do they notice if someone is in the way! Are you all right, mademoiselle? Shall I call for the police?"

"No, we're all right, thank you," Nancy assured him. Inwardly, she was furious. A mobylette had almost hit Keith earlier in the day. A coincidence? Or part of a connected sequence? Did any of the students in Ellen's program have a job delivering pizzas?

The man shrugged and turned away.

"Oh, Nancy, how awful!" George exclaimed.

She was staring down at the ground. The white cardboard box from the bakery lay flattened, with the mark of a tire right across it. A smear of crushed raspberries spread across the pavement.

"Never mind," Nancy said. "Just be glad it was the raspberry tart and not one of us! Come on, let's toss that one and go back for another."

Upstairs, Nancy located the telephone book and studied the list of Pizza Pow! branches. There was one only a few blocks away. "Let's take a look," she suggested to George.

They found the place easily, by the row of mobylettes parked at the curb. As they drew near, a girl in a red jumpsuit and white helmet came out, put a boxed pizza in the metal container on the back of one of the mobylettes, and sped away.

"Look," Nancy said, pausing next to the nearest motorbike. "The keys are in the ignition. Anybody could ride off on one."

"Anyone with nerve," George commented.

They went inside. Two guys and a girl, all in red jumpsuits, were sitting on folding chairs, talking. Behind a counter, an older man was taking an order over the phone. He hung up and turned to Nancy and George.

"You wish to order a pizza?" he asked.

"No," Nancy replied. "You might be interested to know that half an hour ago, we were nearly struck by a Pizza Pow! mobylette."

The man regarded her warily. "We have many deliverers. What was the number of the machine?"

"I don't know," Nancy said. "But the rider was wearing a green coverall and a black helmet."

A look of relief crossed the man's face. "Ah! All of our team wear red jumpsuits and white helmets. Perhaps you mistook the name?"

"No, I saw it clearly," Nancy told him. "Could somebody have, uh, borrowed one of your motorbikes this afternoon?"

"It happens now and then," he admitted. "But not today. Another branch, perhaps?"

After a few more questions, Nancy and George returned to the apartment and began calling other Pizza Pow! agencies. On the third try they found one near the canal St. Martin that had had a mobylette stolen that afternoon. The police had just found it parked near the Bastille.

"The canal St. Martin isn't far from here," George said, studying a city map. "We should get the addresses of people in the exchange program. One of them might live near there."

"Good idea," Nancy replied, making a note. She tried Ellen's number, but she got the answering machine. She left a message explaining what she wanted, then she and George turned their attention to fixing dinner.

That evening they told Carson Drew about their day and what they had discovered.

"The incident with the mobylette makes me think that we're onto something," Nancy concluded. "Unless it was a coincidence, somebody knows we're asking questions about Solo's death and is upset enough to try to frighten us off—or worse."

Nancy's father held up a hand like a traffic cop. "Now hold on," he said. "All you really have at this point is two apparently accidental deaths, possibly linked, and the fact that you were nearly hit by a motorbike. But I was nearly hit today, too, by some idiot on a motorcycle. As far as I'm concerned, the only sane rule in Paris is, assume that anyone on two wheels—and most of those on four wheels—is totally nuts!"

Nancy and George laughed at his vehemence, but then Nancy was quiet for a moment. "Dad, do you really think that our whole investigation is nonsense?" she asked.

"I didn't say that," Carson replied. "But watch out that you don't jump to conclusions."

Nancy promised, and meant it.

After dinner, and helpings of the second raspberry tart, Nancy decided to take a stroll to the Bastille, while George got ready for her date with James. As Nancy left the apartment, David came down the stairs, looking tired.

"Oh, hi," he said. "Are you on your way out? I'm just knocking off my first day of work. You know I'm working for Professor Mathieson now, don't you? I hate to say it, considering the way it happened, but this is a real break for me. It won't be easy, taking Jules's place. He did an amazing amount of work in the last couple of months. If only his notes were better organized. I'm going to end up retracing a lot of what he did."

Nancy wondered. Was David really as callous about the death of Jules as he sounded?

"What are you working on?" she asked.

David rolled his eyes. "Letters, newspaper clippings, checkbooks, old bills, you name it. Solo left all her papers and stuff to Professor Mathieson, you see. There's a stack of cartons in the back room. Some of them have barely been looked at. And they're not in any real order, either. Jules made a start at sorting it out, but there's still a ton to do."

"I'm going for a walk," Nancy said, as they emerged onto the street. "Would you like to join me? I'm headed toward the Bastille."

"Sure, it's on my way home," David replied. "Pam and I are sharing a place over near the canal St. Martin. It's a neat neighborhood, and just a fifteen-minute walk from here."

"Somebody mentioned a good pizza place near there," Nancy said. "It had a funny name—Pizza Pow! Do you know it?"

David shrugged. "Sure, it's just around the corner from us. But it's strictly delivery, and I don't think the pizzas are that great, either."

They turned right. The streets were jammed. In the darkness, the yellow and blue sign for Crédit Lyonnais, a bank, glowed brightly over the sidewalk. At the corner a mobylette zipped by them as they were about to cross the street.

"Those look like fun, don't they," Nancy said brightly. "Have you ever been on one?"

"I've ridden motorcycles back home," David replied. "But the way people drive in this town, I think I'd be too scared to try it here."

Ahead, the glass and white marble facade of the Bastille Opera was brightly lit. At least a hundred people were lounging on the monumental steps that led up to the entrance.

As they walked past one of the bigger cafés that faced the Place de la Bastille, Nancy spotted Pamela at a front row table on the terrace. The guy she was with had his back to Nancy, but it could have been Keith. Nancy glanced over at David. He was staring straight ahead, his face rigid.

"Nancy, David," Pamela called, waving. When Nancy waved back, Pamela gestured to the empty chairs at her table.

"Why don't we join them?" Nancy suggested.

David grunted a reply, but followed her to the table, where he took the seat farthest away from Keith. He sat silently while Nancy and Pamela chatted about Paris, the weather, and what a treat it was to be able to sit at an outdoor café in

November. Then, as the waiter came over to take their orders, David stood up.

"I'm really beat," he announced. "I'm going home and bag some *zzz*'s. See you later."

Pam watched unhappily as her brother walked away. Then she turned to Nancy. "David's pretty stressed about this new job," she said. "It's very important to him to do well at it."

"Don't worry, I understand," Nancy replied. She turned to Keith, "That was a really fun restaurant you took us to today."

A frown crossed Pam's face. Keith must have noticed because he quickly said, "I happened to run into George and Nancy over near the Beaux-Arts at noon." To Nancy, he added, "Glad you liked it. It's a favorite of mine."

Nancy raised an eyebrow. So when Keith and Pamela were together earlier, he hadn't mentioned that he had just had lunch with Nancy and George. Why not?

Keith finished his cup of espresso and pushed his chair back. "I've got a lot of loose ends to tie up," he said, adding, "I don't have any change, Pam. Will you take care of my coffee?"

"Sure," Pam said, but she didn't sound happy.

He cupped her chin in his hand and turned her face toward his. "I'll call you tomorrow," he promised. "Nancy, don't forget about Alain and Didier's party. It should be a blast."

"You know Keith's friends?" Pam asked, as he walked toward the métro entrance.

"Not really," Nancy replied. "One of them came over to our table at lunch and asked us to the party. Are you going?"

Pam began to tear little pieces off her paper napkin. "I don't know . . . A lot of people I know will be there. But Keith asked me to go with him, and David—well . . ." She broke off and stared down at the table.

"Doesn't David like Keith?" asked Nancy.

Pam's cheeks reddened. "He doesn't like me dating him," she admitted. "He says Keith's too old for me, as if it's any business of his. And as if it mattered. There are just a few years' difference, anyway. Keith really knows Paris, he knows all sorts of interesting people, and he likes me a lot. That counts for more than his being a few years older than I, doesn't it?"

"That depends," Nancy said cautiously. "How do you feel about him?"

"I think he's really cute, in a moody kind of way," Pam replied. "And I enjoy going places with him and talking to him about all kinds of things. Isn't that enough? I don't have to fall in love with every guy I go out with, do I?"

"Of course not," Nancy assured her with a laugh. "It sounds to me as if your brother is just a little bit old-fashioned, that's all."

Pam took a deep breath and seemed to relax. "I'm glad I ran into you. For another reason, too. Professor Mathieson told me about what you're doing—investigating what happened to Jules, I mean. And I'd like to help you."

Nancy frowned. "I'm not sure—" she began to say.

"No, wait," Pam said, putting her hand on Nancy's arm. "I feel awful about Jules. If somebody did attack him, it's important that they be caught. But besides that, I've always loved mysteries. I couldn't bear to be in the middle of one and not take part. I'll do whatever you need me to and I won't get in your way. If I do, just tell me to buzz off and I will. Please?"

Nancy thought fast. Pam seemed sincere in her desire to help, and it might be very useful to have someone who was part of the exchange program and knew all the participants. But what if Pam had some less honorable reason for wanting to keep tabs on the case? After all, both her twin brother and current boyfriend were suspects. What if she intended to act as a spy for one or the other of them? In that case, it might be a very shrewd move to have her around, where Nancy and George could keep a close eye on her and discover whether she was spying and for whom.

Nancy took a deep breath. "All right, Pam, you're on," she said. "Why don't you come by our apartment first thing tomorrow? We can have some breakfast and plan our next moves."

"Wow, thanks, Nancy," Pam said, her face

beaming. "I'm psyched! Tell you what—on the way over, I'll pick up fresh croissants."

The next morning Carson had a breakfast meeting. After he left Nancy asked George, "How was your date last night?"

George groaned. "James is very sweet," she replied. "But when he asked me on a walking tour, he really meant it. We must have walked for miles! But it was worth it. Paris is really gorgeous at night, with so many monuments lit up."

The doorbell rang. It was Pam with a bag of croissants. Nancy set the table, while George started a pot of coffee. Then the three girls sat down and enjoyed the rich, flaky pastry.

Nancy carefully wiped her fingers, then leafed through her notes from the day before. "Here's somebody we ought to talk to," she announced. "Phillipe Leduc. His name cropped up several times in Solo's date book, and twice it had exclamation points after it. I couldn't reach him yesterday afternoon, but maybe we'll have better luck today."

"Where does he live?" asked George.

Nancy consulted another page. "On the place du Tertre," she replied. "That sounds familiar."

"Sure," Pam said. "It's that picturesque square up on Montmartre, the old bohemian quarter of Paris. You've probably seen hundreds of paintings of it."

"Well, why don't we take a look at the real thing?" Nancy demanded with a grin.

After calling to make sure that Leduc was in and would talk to them, the three girls made their way to Montmartre. This involved taking the métro, then walking up a winding street, then boarding a cable car that ran up the side of a very steep hill.

"I'm glad we're not doing this on foot," George remarked, gesturing toward the equally steep flight of steps that paralleled the tracks. "Look at the hundreds of steps."

The car bumped to a stop and they got out. The terrace was already crowded with tourists. Some were aiming their cameras and camcorders at the panoramic view of Paris to the south. Others were gaping up at the shining white domes and towers of the church of Sacré-Coeur, built on the highest point in town.

As Nancy and her friends left the cable car station, they found their way blocked by a thick clump of sightseers. Nancy moved to one side and began to edge past them. Suddenly somebody bumped into her, hard. She tried to regain her balance by taking a quick step backward and to the left, but there was nothing under her foot. As she started to fall, she looked over her shoulder and saw, stretching down behind her, the immensely long, steep flight of stone steps.

Chapter Seven

AS SHE FELT HERSELF start to topple backward, Nancy heard cries of alarm from some of the nearby crowd. She twisted her waist and flung her arms out, hoping to grab George or Pam or a total stranger—anyone or anything to save herself from a crippling or even fatal fall. But her friends had walked a few steps ahead, and there was no one near enough. She took a deep breath and tried to prepare herself for the shock.

Suddenly a strong hand closed around her forearm and there was an arm around her waist, keeping her from falling. She groped with her left foot and found the next step down from the terrace. Trembling, she stood upright and looked at her rescuer. To her astonishment, it was David.

"Hey, Nancy, you could have had a nasty fall. What happened?" David asked, still clasping her arm and waist. "Did you get dizzy or something? You should be more careful."

"Somebody in the crowd shoved me," Nancy replied grimly, scanning the faces nearby. She didn't see anyone she knew. "I'm glad you were here to help."

George and Pam rushed back to her side. "Nancy, are you all right?" George demanded.

Nancy nodded. "I'm fine, thanks to David."

Pam stared at her brother. "What on earth are you doing here?" she demanded. "You said you'd be working at Professor Mathieson's."

"I was," he replied. "But I came across something to check out—a copy of a letter from Solo threatening to sue some guy named Leduc for infringing on her rights. His address is near here, on the place du Tertre."

"That's amazing!" Pam said, wide-eyed. "We're just on our way there ourselves!"

"Oh? Why?" David asked in a puzzled voice.

"We're doing some research on Solo, too," Nancy quickly explained. "Leduc was one of the people she had appointments with in her last few months. Do you have that letter you mentioned?"

"No, I left it at the professor's," David replied. He still seemed puzzled, but didn't ask any further questions.

Nancy raised her eyebrows at George. Pam was

right—David's appearance on the scene was an amazing coincidence—if it *was* a coincidence. There were other possibilities, however. David could have followed them, or eavesdropped from Professor Mathieson's apartment when they were on their way out. Or Pam could have told him where they were going and why.

And what about her recent attack? She was pretty sure that it had been deliberate. It was unlikely to be a random assault, especially after that near-miss by the mobylette the night before. No, it seemed as if somebody wanted to scare her off the case, or injure her badly enough to keep her from going on with it. But who?

Perhaps Censier? Or someone working for him? Somebody could have been trailing them the night before, and this morning as well. Nancy resolved to keep a more careful eye out for anyone following them. And what about Leduc? But she quickly dismissed that possibility. After their phone call, he knew they were coming, but not why. And how could he know what Nancy and her friends looked like?

There was one person who had definitely been on the scene this morning, and that was David. And what better way to divert suspicion from himself than to rescue Nancy from an attack that he himself was responsible for?

"Nancy?" George said insistently. "Are you sure you're okay?"

Nancy blinked and glanced around at the

sunny terrace of Sacré-Coeur. The others were staring at her with worried expressions. How long had she been standing there, looking blank and pursuing her thoughts?

"I'm fine," she said firmly. "Let's go find the place du Tertre and Monsieur Leduc."

The address Nancy had written down turned out to be an art gallery. In the window to the left of the door was a painting of two wide-eyed urchins playing on a cobblestone street, with the dome of Sacré-Coeur in the background. It wasn't much different from dozens of paintings Nancy had seen at street fairs back in the States. But in the other window was an ultrarealistic, almost photographic painting of a tabletop, with a coffeepot, cup, and a plateful of toast. It reminded Nancy of the Solo on the wall of Professor Mathieson's apartment, but the signature in the lower right corner read Leduc.

The gallery door was locked. Nancy knocked. After a moment a man came out of the back room. He had a thin, pointed moustache under a sharp nose, and he was wearing a light-colored smock, a blue polka-dot cravat, and a beret.

"I don't believe it," Pam murmured. "He's like a French artist from an old Hollywood movie."

"Yeah," David added, snickering. "A *bad* old Hollywood movie."

The man opened the door wide and said, in a stagy French accent, "Please to entray, ladies and gentleman. In this musée are featured the works of one of the most profound creators of our time, the celebrated Phillipe Leduc."

Nancy looked around. On white-painted brick walls were half a dozen canvases of wide-eyed urchins, an equal number of quaint Paris street scenes, and three in the Solo-like hyperrealist style.

"May we speak to Monsieur Leduc?" Nancy asked. "I called earlier. My name is Nancy Drew."

The man's face fell as he realized that they weren't there to buy a painting. "I'm Leduc," he said. "What can I do for you?"

Nancy said, "We're working on a class project about the life and work of Josephine Solo, and we understand that you knew her well."

"But of course!" Leduc made an expansive gesture with his left arm that nearly hit David in the eye. "Madame Solo was always a source of inspiration to me. She used to say—joking, of course—that I followed her so closely that I stepped on her heels."

"Some of your paintings are very much in her style, aren't they?" David asked in his role as a student of art history. "In fact, that one in the window is close to being an exact copy of one of hers."

Leduc gave David the sort of look he might have given a bug that had just turned up on his dessert. "Great artists have always given homage to other artists in this way," he answered stiffly. "It is a gesture of admiration, nothing more."

Nancy, recalling the letter David had found, asked, "We've heard rumors that Josephine Solo was threatening to sue you. Is that true?"

"Madame Solo was my friend and teacher," Leduc said, continuing in his thick French accent. "Her death was a great loss to me and to the world of art. I can say no more. Now, you will please to excuse me, I am vairy busy man."

He reopened the door and held it while they filed out, then shut and locked it behind them.

"Well!" George exclaimed.

Pam shook her head in disbelief.

"A *very* bad old Hollywood movie," David said, grimacing to keep from exploding in laughter. Then he glanced at his watch and added, "Oops, I'd better dash. I'm supposed to be at the Orsay Museum in just ten minutes. Excuse me, I am vairy busy man!"

The girls chuckled as he hurried off in the direction of the métro. Then Nancy's face sobered as she recalled that David had left the open house early, not long before Jules's accident. Did that mean he had an alibi? Or just the opposite? He did have a possible motive. With Jules out of the way, David stepped into the job that he'd wanted so much. Nancy resolved to question David about that appointment of his the next time she saw him.

"I'd better go, too," Pam said. "I'm supposed to have lunch with a school friend who's here for a few days. Can I link up with you guys later? I'll give you a call."

"Great," Nancy replied.

As Pam, too, started toward the métro, Nancy wondered about her as well. She had been so insistent about helping with the investigation. But after one interview, she made an excuse to leave. Was the excuse genuine? Then why hadn't Pam mentioned a lunch date before? Maybe detective work simply wasn't as thrilling as she had expected, but she was too polite to say so. Or maybe she was the kind of person who fluttered from one interest to another, easily losing enthusiasm when she didn't see instant results.

"What did you think of that guy Leduc?" George asked, as she and Nancy paused at the corner to let a tour bus go by.

"A genuine tin-plated phony," Nancy said promptly. "And he was certainly stealing ideas from Solo, and she knew it and was threatening to take action. Her death was very convenient for him. But I don't think that means he killed her. At worst, he would have had to stop copying her and start copying some other famous artist."

"Yes, but— Oh, Nancy, look," George said.

One of the many sidewalk artists who were installed around the sides of the square had done a lightning sketch of Nancy and was displaying it to the small crowd that had gathered to watch.

Catching her eye, he motioned to the folding chair next to his easel.

"Please, I will do in pastels for free," he said. "Only because you are so beautiful. If you do not like enough to buy, I keep as a souvenir."

The many eyes turned on her made Nancy's cheeks grow warm. "No, thank you," she said, shaking her head and smiling.

"Oh, go on," George whispered to her.

"No, I couldn't, really," Nancy whispered back. "I want to go back to the apartment and try to set up appointments with the people still on our list. We also need to contact the police. I'd like to know what they made of Jules's death, and whether his briefcase ever turned up."

As she and George turned to leave, the artist rolled up his sketch of Nancy and presented it to her with a bow. "To remember Paris," he said.

Nancy knew that she would, with great fondness.

When they reached the apartment, Nancy found a note from her father.

Nan—

Call Professor Mathieson as soon as you get in. She says it's important but not urgent.

I have a business dinner and have to go to the theater this evening, but what do you and George think about brunch tomorrow?

Dad

Nancy showed the note to George, then went to the telephone.

"I've stumbled across something rather odd," Ellen said, after Nancy identified herself. "I'd like to know what you and George think of it. Can you come up now?"

Upstairs, the professor led Nancy and George into her office at the back of the apartment. Cardboard cartons were stacked against one wall, and the desk—a door supported by two sawhorses—was cluttered with papers.

"I don't know if I told you that Jo had very little money in the bank when she died," Ellen said. "That always puzzled me. Her works sold for very handsome prices, after all. This morning I decided to try to find out where the money went. Unfortunately, French banks don't send back your cancelled checks, but I did manage to locate Jo's most recent checkbook. Here, take a look and see if anything strikes you."

George peeked over Nancy's shoulder as she leafed through the check stubs. Finally Nancy closed the checkbook and said, "During the last few months of her life, every time money came into her account, Solo immediately wrote a large check—anywhere from six thousand to almost thirty thousand francs—to someone called G.A. Who is G.A.?"

"I have no idea," Ellen replied. "I haven't been able to think of anyone with those initials among her acquaintances. And I know of no one to whom Jo would have willingly given practically every cent she had."

"Willingly," Nancy repeated slowly. "There's another possibility, though. One that probably occurred to you, too. Maybe she didn't give the money willingly. Maybe Josephine Solo was in the clutches of a blackmailer."

Chapter Eight

BLACKMAIL!" George exclaimed. The word hung in the air like a dark, ominous cloud. "But who would blackmail Solo, and over what?"

"We obviously don't know," Nancy replied. "Somebody who knew something about her that she didn't want the rest of the world to know."

"There was never a breath of scandal about Jo," Ellen said. "She was devoted to her work. You could almost say that her work *was* her life. I would never have picked her as a likely target for a blackmailer."

"She was paying practically everything she had to this G.A.," Nancy pointed out. "Can you think of a better explanation than blackmail?"

George said, "Maybe she had a sick relative with huge medical bills. Or maybe her mother was in a nursing home."

Ellen shook her head. "Jo's parents have been dead for years, and she was an only child. She had no close relations at all. I suppose she could have been giving the money to someone to invest for her," she added. "But in that case, the person would have come forward after Jo died."

"If he or she was honest," George said. "But what if she was the victim, not of a blackmailer, but of a con artist? You know—'Invest in my diamond mines and double your money.'"

"Good thinking, George," Nancy said. "That makes a lot of sense."

"Ye-e-s," George replied hesitantly. "Except for one thing. I've heard stories of desperate victims killing a blackmailer, but I never heard of a blackmailer killing his victim. Or a con artist, either. The whole point is to keep the victim alive and paying."

"True. But what if you turn on him and threaten to expose him?" Nancy asked. "A hardened, desperate criminal might go to any extreme to silence you, even if it meant pushing you in front of a truck. But here's something else. Gail Fountain thought Solo might have been involved in a romance. What if her new partner was the one she was giving all her money to, and she decided to break it off?"

Ellen was looking back and forth between George and Nancy. "I can see that Bob wasn't exaggerating when he talked about your detective talent," she remarked. "This is an education for me. But I don't know about Jo's being involved with anyone. I think I would have, though goodness knows she was fond of keeping secrets. And the police thought that Jo's death was an accident. I have a copy of their report in my files. What if they were right? I know I said I thought it might not be, but what if? Doesn't that destroy your theory?"

Nancy shook her head. "Not at all. Solo was practically broke when she died, thanks to those payments to G.A. What if she was being driven frantic by demands she couldn't meet? Or by the fear of finding herself penniless?"

Ellen was shocked. "Surely you're not suggesting that Jo deliberately stepped in front of that truck," she gasped.

"It's a possibility," Nancy replied. "But even if she didn't, her state of mind could have made her less careful than usual. And in that case, it seems to me that the person who helped create that state of mind bears a lot of the responsibility for her death."

"Nancy?" George said. "Do you think this is the amazing discovery that Jules made, that Solo was being bled white by someone? Jules might even have managed to find out who G.A. really is."

"But died under the wheels of a truck before he could pass on the information," Nancy added. "Yes, George, I'd call that our strongest theory at this point. But what we really need isn't another theory, it's more evidence. And for a start, I'd like to have a clearer picture of Josephine Solo's death. It happened somewhere near here, didn't it?" she asked Ellen.

The professor nodded. "That's right—at the corner of the rue de Charonne and the rue Leon Frot. They're both pretty narrow, and the rue de Charonne is a very busy street. I'm surprised there aren't more accidents there."

"Were there any witnesses?" Nancy asked.

"There must have been," Ellen replied. "But the police report doesn't give their names."

Nancy drummed her fingers on the desk. "Would you see if you can put your hands on that report?" she asked. "Meanwhile, I'd like to ask around near the place where it happened. It's not all that long ago. People might still remember."

"I'll do that. And please let me know what you find out," the professor replied. "Jo was my good friend. If she was in the grip of some evil person, I want to know about it. Nothing will bring her back, but at least I could tell the person what I think of him."

Nancy and George stopped in the apartment to leave a note for Carson telling him where they were going. Then they set off to follow George's map to the intersection of the rue de Charonne and the rue Leon Frot. Their route took them along quiet side streets lined with old stone buildings. Some had freshly cleaned facades and new windows. Others looked as if they hadn't been maintained since they were built a hundred years earlier. From one of the courtyards came the high-pitched whine of a power saw and the sharp, tangy smell of sawdust. The window of a nearby shop displayed hundreds of intricate brass fittings for fine furniture. Nancy would have liked to go more slowly and explore, but the investigation was more important than sightseeing.

The rue de Charonne was as narrow and busy as Ellen had said. As Nancy and George turned onto it, a green city bus sped by only inches from the curb. The front tire hit a puddle, sending a sheet of water onto the sidewalk. Nancy jumped back just in time. George wasn't so quick. She first glared at her soaked shoes and socks, then at the bus.

"You'd think the driver could show some consideration and slow down a little," she said. "And what was that water doing in the gutter anyway? It hasn't rained since we got here."

As if in answer, a tiny green truck appeared at the corner on the sidewalk, and rolled slowly toward them, spraying jets of water at the concrete. Two men in green coveralls walked behind it, sweeping the walk with green plastic brooms. The girls ducked into a doorway and waited for it to pass, then walked on to rue Leon Frot.

Nancy studied the small shops that lined the

street on either side. With so many shops, surely someone in one of them had seen what happened to Josephine Solo.

"Let's start at the corner and work our way down the block, then back up the other side," she suggested to George.

The store on the corner was a bakery with a long line of customers waiting to buy fresh bread for lunch. "Why don't we try the optician next door?" George suggested.

Inside the optician's shop, a young woman in a white lab coat asked the girls if she could be of help.

Nancy explained in French that they were searching for people who might have witnessed a fatal accident on the corner earlier in the year.

"The poor woman who was crushed by the truck, you mean?" the woman replied. "But, of course, everyone in the *quartier* knows about that. And later we learned that she was a famous artist. It is scandalous the way the trucks and buses speed down such a small, crowded street. Only last week, my son, who is nine, was nearly hit by an immense tourist bus from England."

"You saw the accident in which Josephine Solo was killed?" George asked eagerly. "Can you tell us exactly what happened?"

The woman pursed her lips, then said, "I did not see it happen. I was with a client at the time. But I heard the noises of brakes and the screams. And when I ran to the window, I saw the poor woman's legs sticking out from under the truck. One of her shoes had been knocked off. I could tell that there was no hope."

Nancy and George asked a few more questions, but it was clear that the woman had not actually seen what happened. Nor did she know anyone who had. They thanked her and went on to the next shop, which sold fruits and vegetables. The owner, in a stained white apron, remembered the incident well. He had been standing with his back to the street, arranging a pyramid of artichokes, when he heard the crash. He had turned instantly.

"Was there anyone near the victim?" asked Nancy.

The man raised both his bushy eyebrows. "But of course! Everyone was running to help. I, too. When I did my military service, I had to learn some first aid. But this time it was useless. There was nothing to be done."

Nancy and George canvassed half a dozen more stores, then crossed the street—carefully checking both ways—and canvassed the stores on that side. When they finally made it back to the corner, George and Nancy were discouraged.

"The same story everywhere!" George exclaimed. "Everyone looked only moments after the accident, but no one saw it happen. I'm beginning to think they're all in it together."

Nancy felt the same as George, but she refused to give up. She glanced around, hoping for inspiration, and noticed a man in green coveralls with a broom with green plastic bristles. He knelt down and inserted a metal tool into a slot in the sidewalk, then turned it. Water gushed into the street, and he began to sweep litter into the gutter.

Nancy went over to him. "Excuse me. Have you been working in this area for long?" she asked in French.

He straightened up and gave her a long look. "For two years. Why?"

"Were you by any chance here last spring, the day an American woman was hit by a truck?" Nancy continued, then held her breath waiting for his reply.

"Ah, *alors!*" he exclaimed. "But of course I was here. I saw it all—all!"

"Exactly what happened?" Nancy asked.

The street sweeper put down his broom, the better to gesticulate, and said, "Look you, I was preparing to turn on the water when I saw the woman on the sidewalk, going to the corner. Aha, I think. I'll wait a moment, not to wet her feet. So I am watching her. She walks to the corner, her eyes on nothing in particular. But then—imagine—then she turns her head, like this. To look back at a shop window? Or a passerby who seems familiar? I don't know. Then without looking, she steps into the street, directly in front of the truck. *Quel horreur!*"

Chapter Nine

NANCY STARED at the street sweeper. "You were watching the woman at the very moment she stepped into the street?" she demanded. "You saw the whole thing?"

"Did I not just say that?" he replied, with a shrug of his shoulders.

"Was there anyone near her?" George asked, also in French. "Anyone who might have, uh, distracted her?"

He wagged his finger. "No, no, no. I told the police at the time, now I tell you. I was the closest, and I was three meters away, too far to help, *hélas!*"

Nancy mentally translated this as about ten feet. "Then you don't have any doubt that it was an accident," she said.

"No doubt at all," he replied, bending down to

pick up his broom again. "A tragic accident, *c'est tout.*"

Nancy thanked him for his help, then she and George went to a nearby café to talk about what this meant.

"Nancy, I feel really confused," George admitted after they ordered a coffee and a tea with milk. "We've been basing our whole investigation on the premise that Solo was murdered. If she wasn't—and that guy's testimony was pretty convincing—then everything we've done so far was one big waste of time."

Nancy put her elbows on the table, rested her chin on her folded hands, and gazed out through the café window at the street. Was George right? Had they spent the last two days chasing a phantom?

"Not quite," she said slowly. "Okay, Solo's death was an accident. But what about Jules? At least one witness thought he was pushed under the truck. And *somebody* stole that briefcase of his."

"But we haven't even started investigating Jules's death," George protested. "We've been investigating *Solo's.*"

"On the theory that the two were connected," Nancy pointed out. She paused as the waiter set their drinks on the table, then continued. "I still think it's a good theory. Jules was doing research on Solo's last months and told Ellen he'd just made an amazing discovery. But before he could meet her to share his discovery, he was killed."

George nodded. "And the briefcase he was carrying vanished—and it probably contained his notes on the discovery," she added. "Okay, I get the point. Whatever Jules discovered, it must have been terribly incriminating for someone, someone who had had a connection to Josephine Solo. Maybe someone like Censier or that guy Leduc, who was apparently copying her ideas."

"Don't forget G.A., who may have been blackmailing her," Nancy said. "And another thing—even if Solo's death was an accident, it may have inspired the person who killed Jules to copy it. After all, if you shoot or poison somebody, everybody knows it's murder. But if somebody stumbles in front of a truck, there's a good chance people will think it was an accident, and you won't have to face an investigation."

"Unless you have bad luck and cross the path of Nancy Drew and Company," George declared with a mock-fierce expression. "Okay, so where do we go from here?"

Nancy frowned. "Let's go on assuming that the reason Jules died had something to do with his discovery about Solo," she said. "If we can manage to retrace his steps and find out what he discovered, maybe it will point us in the direction of his killer. We should also try to find out how the killer found out about the discovery, and how he knew that Jules was on his way to Ellen's."

"We should start checking people's alibis, too," George suggested. "And not just for the time Jules was killed. Don't forget that mobylette that tried to run us down or the attack on you this morning."

Nancy stood up. "I'm going to try to reach Ellen," she said. "Maybe she can tell us where Jules was living. If we can get into his apartment, we might find a clue to what he found."

Nancy returned to the table a few minutes later, smiling. "Good news," she announced. "Jules was renting a spare room in the apartment of a friend of Ellen who's a professor at the Sorbonne. I have the address. It's over on the Left Bank, near the Luxembourg Gardens. Ellen's going to call and ask to let us see Jules's room."

"Great," George said. She unfolded her map and scanned it, then added, "Oh, good—we can take a bus there. It's much more fun to be able to look out at the streets along the way."

The apartment was on a quiet side street, just a few steps from the Sorbonne and the bustling boulevard St. Michel. Nancy rang the bell. The man who answered was in his fifties, with steel-gray hair and a closely trimmed gray beard.

"Miss Drew, Miss Fayne?" he said, with an English accent. "I'm Pierre Reuilly. Please come in. Ellen Mathieson told me to expect you."

Nancy and George followed him into the living room. The walls were lined with ceiling-high bookcases of dark wood. An impressive antique desk stood at the far end between two tall French windows.

"We're sorry to intrude on you," Nancy said.

"Oh, not at all. I understand you wish to look through poor Daubenton's affairs," Reuilly replied. "You arrive at an opportune moment. I was planning to pack everything this weekend, to ship to his family in Burgundy."

"Do you have any idea what research he was doing for Ellen?" Nancy asked.

Reuilly shook his head. "That, I fear, I do not know. In view of what happened, I feel quite bad that I didn't get to know the chap better, but our paths rarely crossed. You'll understand the reason when I show you his quarters. This way."

Nancy and George followed him down a long, dark hall with closed doors on both sides. At the end, was a large, old-fashioned kitchen.

Reuilly pointed to a door near the refrigerator and said, "That leads onto the rear stairs. In the last century, when this building was put up, it was not considered proper for servants to use the same entrance as their employers. I never use this back entrance, but I gave Daubenton the keys so that he could come and go as he wished without having to run into me constantly. You can understand that we rarely saw each other. His room is just over here."

The professor pushed open a narrow door at the far end of the kitchen and added, "I'll leave you, then. If I can be of further service, you'll find me in my study."

"One question, if you don't mind," Nancy quickly said. "Has anyone else come by to look at his room? A friend or relative, maybe? Or the police?"

"No, no one at all," Reuilly told her. "His relatives asked me to send his belongings, but I haven't had time yet. Poor chap, it's such a terrible thing that happened."

The room Jules had occupied was small and rather barren. A single bed took up most of one wall. Along the opposite wall were an armoire, a bookcase whose shelves sagged under their load, and a desk made of two sawhorses and a wide plank. The uncurtained window framed a view of the roof of the next building.

"Brrr!" George said, pretending to shiver. "And he was an art history major. You'd think he could have put a few prints on the walls to cheer the place up."

Nancy said, "I suspect he was the kind of person who doesn't really notice his surroundings. He had a place to work, a place to sleep, and a place to store his stuff. What else did he need?

"Well, let's get to work," Nancy added after a pause. "You take the bookcase. I'll start on the desk."

George began taking books down, shaking

each one, in case a paper was tucked inside, and examining the titles. Nancy approached the desk. Jules had obviously tried to be organized—four cardboard box files were stacked on the floor near the desk—but he hadn't quite managed. Most of the desk's surface was hidden by piles of file folders, paper clipped sheafs of notes, letters, magazines, and stray scraps of paper.

Holding back a sigh, Nancy started sorting through the papers, setting aside any that might relate to Josephine Solo. When she finished, she had compiled a stack over an inch thick that seemed to deserve closer scrutiny. One item that she spent a long time perusing was a notebook in which each page was headed with a date, starting about a year earlier. The majority of the pages were blank, but others contained anything from a single word to a whole paragraph. After studying it, Nancy decided that the notebook was a summary of the research Jules had been doing into the daily life of Josephine Solo.

She selected one of the longer entries, from late November, and read.

> Replied EM's letter 14.11 re grant (corres files). Met pm w/ J-LC, broke off w/ gallery. Din 2Mag w/ GFountain.

That was easy enough to decode. EM was Ellen, J-LC was Censier, and GFountain was the food writer whom Nancy and George had interviewed the day before. So after breaking off relations with the gallery that had represented her for years, Solo had celebrated, or consoled herself, by having dinner with a close friend at the Deux Magots.

Nancy leafed through the notebook again, copying any entries that seemed relevant, but she didn't note anything that ranked as an amazing discovery. Of course not, because Jules had certainly taken his documents to show Ellen, and they were now in the hands of the person who had stolen his briefcase. Or had destroyed it.

"I've drawn a total blank," George said, breaking into Nancy's thoughts. "How about you?"

"I'm not doing so well, either," Nancy replied, continuing through the stack of papers. "But what was I expecting? A hot pink folder labeled Important Clue? Whatever Jules—"

She broke off as something caught her eye. It was a scrap of paper with a column of numbers. Something about the numbers looked familiar.

6250
14000
11500
8000
28500

"What is it, Nan?" asked George, coming over to stand by the desk.

Nancy showed her the paper. "Aren't those the amounts of the checks Solo wrote to G.A.?"

"Yes," George replied, excitement in her voice. "All except that one at the bottom."

Nancy read, "CL 381–44961210—No, that certainly doesn't ring a bell. But I'm going to copy this list. When we get home, we can compare it with the amounts of those checks. If they match, it means that Jules was on the trail of the blackmailer."

Nancy spent the next twenty minutes going through the rest of the papers, while George searched Jules's clothes. Neither of them found anything else that resembled a clue. Finally they thanked Professor Reuilly and returned home.

As they were going upstairs, Nancy said, "I'd like to look at that checkbook now. Let's see if Ellen is in."

They continued up another flight and knocked on her door. It was David who answered. "No, the professor's out," he said. "She said she'd be back around five. Boy, this research business is a lot harder than I thought it would be. I'm just beginning to find my way around."

Nancy decided this was a good moment to begin checking alibis. "David?" she said. "You remember that on Thursday night, you left the party before us?"

"Yes," he said, in a guarded voice. "What about it?"

"Would you mind telling me why?"

He glared at her. "Playing detective? Well, I would mind, but I'll tell you anyway. I went to meet somebody. But the guy I was supposed to meet didn't show up. I wasted half an hour standing around."

"Alone?" George asked.

"Yes, alone," he replied, sticking his chin out. "What of it?"

"Who were you expecting to meet?" Nancy probed. "Any idea why he failed to show up?"

David suddenly became uneasy. "Sure," he said. "I know exactly why. Because he'd just been killed by a truck. The guy I was supposed to meet was Jules Daubenton."

Chapter Ten

NANCY FELT as if someone had just touched an ice cube to the back of her neck. David was admitting that he had an appointment to meet Jules at the very time that Jules died.

There was an uneasy silence in the room. David's eyes shifted from Nancy to George and back, as if he were dreading their reactions.

George cleared her throat and said, "I don't get it. Why were you and Jules supposed to meet?"

"I don't know," David growled. "It wasn't my idea, it was his. He said it was important, that's all I know."

Nancy frowned. There was something here that didn't add up. Why would Jules make a date to meet David for the same time that he was rushing to an urgent appointment with Professor Mathieson?

"When did Jules ask you to meet him?" Nancy asked.

"I don't know," David said again, with a scowl. "During Professor Mathieson's open house, that's all I know. Look, here's what happened. Near the end of the open house, Cindy—you remember, the brown-haired girl from Oklahoma?—brought me a message that Jules had called. He said he needed to see me and would meet me in front of the bookstore over on Ledru Rollin at ten o'clock. I probably wouldn't have bothered, but he said it was important."

"Did he tell Cindy why it was so important?" asked George.

David gave an exasperated sigh. "That's the whole point," he said. "She didn't talk to him. She just found the message next to the telephone and brought it to me."

"Let me see if I've got this straight," Nancy said. "Somebody answered the telephone and took down a message for you from Jules. And then, instead of giving it to you, he or she simply left it by the telephone? Even though it was supposed to be very important?"

"Look, I know it sounds fishy," David said, raising his voice. "All I can say is, I didn't think anything about it at the time. I just figured whoever took the call got distracted and forgot to give me the note."

George said, "David, I don't understand why you didn't tell anybody about this."

"You mean, after I found out that Jules had been killed?" he retorted. "And that he had been on his way to meet with Professor Mathieson, not with me? Give me a break! That message wasn't from Jules at all. Somebody was trying to set me up. Why make it easier for them?"

"Do you still have the note?" Nancy asked. "Maybe the handwriting—"

"No such luck," he said bitterly. "I tossed it in a litter basket on my way to meet Jules."

George asked, "Who can confirm your story?"

"It's not a story, it's what happened," he burst out. "Cindy can. She'll certainly remember giving me the note. She even made a joke about playing postman."

"Yes, but what about the time you spent in front of the bookstore," George continued. "Did you see anybody you know?"

David's face turned red. "That is such a dumb question, George. How many times do *you* run into somebody you know on the street? Once a month? And I've only been in this town since September. No, I didn't see anybody I knew."

"Hey, take it easy," Nancy told him. "We're not out to get you. We simply want to find out what happened."

"I'm sorry," David mumbled. "But I've had this thing hanging over me ever since Pam told me about Jules. It's a relief to tell you about it, even if you don't believe me. Er—does Professor Mathieson have to hear about this?"

"We can't promise to keep it secret," Nancy replied. "But we're not into gossip."

"I guess that's all I can hope for," he said gloomily. "Why did this happen to me?"

"What happened to you isn't as bad as what happened to Jules," George reminded him.

David was struck silent before he turned away. "You'd better go now," he said. "There's nothing else I can tell you, and I've got a lot of work to finish." He went back inside.

Nancy caught George's eye and nodded toward the stairs. "Let's take a look at the checkbook later," she whispered to George. "Right now I want to talk."

Back in their apartment, George led the way to the living room and sank onto the sofa. "What do you make of David's story?" she asked.

Nancy fiddled with the flowers on the mantel while she sorted out her thoughts. "I don't believe for a moment that Jules called up and left that message for David. Why would he do that, at a time when he was rushing to his meeting with Professor Mathieson? He and David weren't even friends. Just the opposite if anything. And remember, when we saw Jules, just before the accident, he was headed in this direction. The avenue de Ledru Rollin is in the opposite direction. So Jules was not on his way to a rendezvous with David."

"Then you think David made up the whole thing?" George pursued.

"Not necessarily," Nancy said. She crossed to the window and peered out. The sky overhead was still blue, but to the east was a bank of dark gray clouds.

"There must have been a note, for one thing," she continued. "David wouldn't have dared invent that. We'd learn he was lying the minute we asked this girl, Cindy, about it."

"But he could have written the note himself, then left it by the telephone for somebody to find," George pointed out.

"I know, I thought of that," Nancy told her. "But look at it this way. Suppose David overheard the phone call Jules made to Professor Mathieson and decided, for whatever reason, to ambush Jules before he got here. And then he decided to construct a phony alibi for the time of the planned ambush. Okay so far?"

George studied Nancy's face suspiciously. "It could have been that way," she said.

Nancy nodded. "Sure, it could have been. But if David were trying to give himself an alibi, why on earth did he invent a story that *isn't* an alibi? Not to mention a story that links him directly with Jules?"

"When you put it that way," George said, "it doesn't make much sense, does it? Unless he expected us to reason like that. In that case, the fact that it makes him seem innocent is really evidence that he's guilty."

Nancy picked up a pillow from the sofa and

tossed it at George. "With reasoning like that, you can prove that I'm the queen of England!"

She glanced at her watch, then stood up and crossed to the telephone. "I hope there's time to get in touch with the local gendarmes before the offices close."

After twenty minutes of being switched from one extension to another, each time explaining what she wanted, Nancy replaced the receiver and sighed out loud.

"Jules's death is recorded as an accident," she reported to George. "And his briefcase hasn't turned up. I tried to tell the guy in charge about what's been happening, but he didn't sound very interested. He told me to come in on Monday and fill out a report. Until we come up with some solid evidence, we're obviously on our own."

"Do you think this is wild enough for a studio party?" George demanded.

George had burgundy tights on under a long navy blue tunic, with a burgundy-colored scarf tied at her waist. Her dark, curly hair was caught up off center with a blue enamel clip.

"You look terrific," Nancy assured her, and went back to examining her own image in the mirror of the armoire. She had chosen shiny black stirrup pants and a burnt-orange blouse. Now she was wondering if the blouse clashed with her reddish blond hair. With a decisive gesture, she switched the blouse for a white one, topped it with a big purple sweater, and pulled on a pair of purple suede ankle boots.

"I'm set," she announced, after a last look in the mirror.

Nancy and George left the apartment and walked past the place de la Bastille to the Seine. Just across the river was the Latin Quarter, called that since the days when university students and professors spoke Latin among themselves. The girls strolled slowly through the narrow, winding streets, stopping occasionally to window shop or admire a view.

Didier's studio was in an old building in a stone-paved courtyard. They could hear the noise of the party the moment they went in and started up the worn stairs.

The studio, on the top floor, was one big room with a ceiling that rose up to fifteen or twenty feet. Three huge pink kites shaped like fish dangled from the top rafter and swayed in the currents of air. Through one of the windows, Nancy caught a distant glimpse of the upper section of the floodlit Eiffel Tower.

Alain noticed them and came over. "Welcome," he said. "You are Keith's friends, no? He never told me your names."

Nancy and George introduced themselves. Alain called over a short guy with long, sandy-colored hair and pale blue eyes. This was Didier, the other host of the party.

"Nice to meet you," he said. "Refreshments are over by the window. Have fun."

As he drifted away, Pam hurried over. "George! Nancy!" she said. "I was starting to think you weren't coming. Listen, what happened to you? I tried to call all afternoon. You must think I flaked out on you this morning, but I'd already put off that lunch twice. Frankly, I would rather have stayed and helped you."

Nancy smiled politely, but she couldn't help recalling her earlier suspicions of Pam.

Keith joined them, nodding hello. He had dressed up for the party, adding a pair of black leather wristbands to his usual black shirt, jeans, vest, and boots.

"Tonight you'll get an inside look at the real Bohemian life—*la vie de Bohème,"* he said, waving to indicate the party-goers in the studio. As if on cue, an accordionist in the corner began to play a bouncy tune in three-four time. Keith wordlessly grabbed Pam and danced off with her.

Nancy glanced across the room. David was standing rigidly, staring at Keith and Pam, his features set in a grim expression tinged with strong dislike. His eyes shifted and he noticed Nancy watching him. An expression of alarm crossed his face and then he gave her a thin smile.

"George, hi!" A tall, thin guy with a boyish smile and a lock of dark hair falling across his forehead came up to them. His T-shirt was from a folkdance festival in Ontario. After a moment,

Nancy placed him—James, who had taken George on the walking tour of town.

"Hey, let's dance," he said to George after giving Nancy a smile and a nod. "This is a dance from the twenties called the java. Come on, I'll teach you. It's easy and loads of fun."

"I'll try," George said, laughing. "But no promises."

As the party continued, Nancy danced a couple of times with Alain, once with Didier, and even one time with Keith, who stared at her intently the whole time. He walked away without a word when the music ended. She also met a lot of people, including a chain-smoking art-rock composer who wanted to move to New York, an architecture student from a former French colony in central Africa, and two American girls who seemed uncomfortable and out of place.

Through it all, Nancy kept an eye on Keith, Pam, and David. The pattern set at the beginning of the party continued. Keith was always in the thick of things, with Pam in his wake, and David glaring at them. Finally Pam took her twin aside and evidently gave him a talking-to. The next time Nancy looked for David, she didn't see him, and she concluded he had left the party. Pam acted unhappy but relieved.

At about one o'clock, Pam approached Nancy and George. "Keith's meeting some people at a jazz club," she said, "but I want to go home. It's too late for the métro. Want to share a taxi?"

"Sure. I'm ready to go," Nancy replied.

George turned pink. "James asked me to go dancing after the party."

"Oh? Fine, have fun," Nancy said. "You have your keys and the code for the downstairs door?"

"Sure," George replied. "See you later."

Nancy and Pam found Didier and Alain, thanked them, then left. The streets were still crowded and lively. They paused to watch a street mime, then hunted up a taxi rank.

The ride to Pam's house took surprisingly little time. "Some of the people in the exchange program are planning a picnic tomorrow afternoon at Vincennes," Pam offered as she was getting out. "If you and George want to come, why not give me a call in the morning?"

"I'll do that," Nancy promised.

Five minutes later the taxi stopped in front of Nancy's building. She paid the driver, then stepped out, locating in her purse the slip of paper where she'd written the door code. She used the keypad on the wall to let herself into the darkened courtyard. She was just reaching for the button that turned on the courtyard lights when an arm grasped her neck. Choking, she felt herself being dragged backward, deep into the shadows.

Chapter Eleven

NANCY TRIED to call for help, but the attacker tightened his stranglehold on her and dragged her toward a dark corner of the courtyard.

Once her initial moment of shock passed, Nancy began to think quickly and coolly. She knew it was useless to try to pull the arm off her neck. Her attacker had the leverage in his favor. No, in order to free herself she needed a moment to regain her balance. And for that, she needed to get him off balance.

A kung-fu move she had once learned came back to her. Clasping her right fist in her left hand for added power, she drove the point of her right elbow backward, into her attacker's midsection. He gave a grunt of pain and surprise, and his arm around Nancy's neck loosened slightly.

Instantly Nancy took his forearm in both hands,

fell to one knee, and executed a perfect shoulder throw. As her assailant hit the ground, she sprang up and aimed a kick at him.

"Ow!"

The kick had obviously connected. Nancy moved in to deliver another, but the frustrated assailant jumped up, shoved her aside, and ran. Taken by surprise, Nancy was a second late in pursuing him. As he tugged open the door to the street, she caught a glimpse of him, but all she could tell was that he was of average height and build. The hood pulled down low over his face kept her from making out his features.

As Nancy reached the door, she heard the sound of a mobylette speeding off. By the time she got to the sidewalk, it was out of sight, but she was ready to bet that it had a Pizza Pow! box on the back.

Nancy rubbed her neck and swallowed a couple of times before going upstairs to telephone the police. An officer took her statement over the phone and promised an investigation, but pointed out that the assailant had already escaped. Before hanging up, he apologized to her on behalf of France.

On the dining room table, Nancy found a note from her father. He had turned in early but wanted to remind them of their brunch date the next morning. Nancy considered waking him to tell him about the attack, then decided it could wait until morning. She found a notepad and pen and curled up on the sofa to plot out the next steps in her investigation.

"Nan, how awful!" George exclaimed, wide-eyed. It was ten A.M., and Nancy, who had been up for a couple of hours, had just told her friend about the attack on her.

"That means those earlier attacks weren't just coincidence," George continued. "We must really be bothering somebody."

"Somebody who knew about what time I'd get home and who also knew the door code," Nancy pointed out.

"Nancy?" George said. "I hate to say it, but there's at least one suspect who knows the door code. Ellen's new research assistant—David."

"I thought of that," Nancy replied. "But I called Ellen this morning. All the students in the exchange program were told the door code last month, when she held an evening meeting here. And it's possible that whoever attacked me *didn't* know it, that he waited outside and slipped in when somebody went in or out."

Carson's bedroom door opened and he appeared, already dressed. "What?" he said in mock astonishment. "Still in pajamas, at this hour? Time's a-wasting!"

Nancy and George hurried off to dress. When they returned, Carson telephoned for a taxi. "It's not an extravagance," he explained cheerfully. "There's no métro station close to where we're going, and most buses don't run on Sunday. With three of us a cab's probably the best way to go, anyway."

The taxi crossed to the Left Bank, then took a ramp that went down to the quay, the paved embankment along the river. The driver came to a halt next to a brightly painted canal barge that was moored in the shadow of Notre Dame Cathedral.

"Is this where we're having brunch?" Nancy asked.

"It is indeed," Carson replied. He led her and George over the gangplank, onto the deck of the barge. The main cabin had wide windows on both sides, the whole length. The widely spaced tables were set with sparkling china and silver, but they were the only customers.

A smiling woman in a flowered skirt and white blouse led them to a table next to a window with a view directly across the water to the towering Gothic cathedral.

"This place is really special," Nancy commented as the woman brought a basket of bread and croissants, a dish of butter, and jars of jam and honey, before going back for a tray of coffee, tea, heated milk, and chilled orange juice.

As Nancy was buttering her croissant, her father said, "I'm sorry you two couldn't have been at the theater with me last night. The actors were sensational. But how did you enjoy your studio party?"

"The party was a lot of fun," Nancy replied. "But the sequel wasn't." She told her father about the attack on her in the courtyard of the building.

"Nancy," he said gravely. "You know I don't believe in interfering in your work, but I'd be neglecting my duty as a father if I didn't warn you to be more careful. You're obviously dealing with a desperate person."

"He has a right to be a little desperate," Nancy replied. "We're starting to close in on him." She told her father about the note David had supposedly received from Jules, and why she was sure that it hadn't been from Jules.

"I see your point," Carson said. "But in that case, and if there wasn't a call from Jules, then who wrote that note, and why?"

"Unless David did it himself, his own explanation is the most obvious one," Nancy said thoughtfully. "Somebody tried to set him up by making sure that he didn't have an alibi for the time Jules was expected to arrive at the professor's."

"So whoever killed Jules must have been one of the people at the open house," George commented. "So it couldn't have been Censier or Leduc or whoever may have been blackmailing Solo. We've been searching in the wrong direction the whole time."

"Not necessarily," Nancy replied. "Someone who was at the party may be working with

Censier or Leduc or G.A. in whatever their scheme is. Our Mr. or Ms. X overheard Ellen's phone call from Jules, realized that it threatened the scheme, and either alerted his partner or decided to take action on his own. Roping in David by way of that note was just an extra flourish to confuse the trail."

The barge rocked gently as a glass-roofed sightseeing boat went by twenty feet from them in the narrow channel. A couple of the tourists aboard aimed their cameras at Nancy, George, and Carson. George smiled and waved, then turned back to Nancy. "Then you don't think it was David who attacked you last night?" she asked.

Nancy frowned. "It could have been," she said slowly. "I can't tell you why I'm so sure that it wasn't. But somehow, I am."

"A day or two ago you thought he might be capable of pushing Jules in front of a truck in order to take over the job," Carson pointed out. "Now you've changed your opinion. Why?"

Nancy leaned back in her chair and fiddled with the handle of her coffee cup. "I don't really know," she said at last. "And I'm not crossing him off my list of suspects, but if he turns out to be guilty, I'll be surprised."

Carson smiled grimly. "Every time someone commits a particularly grisly crime, the news cameras find dozens of neighbors and friends who say how surprised they are. To me, all that means is that people are too easily surprised."

"Dad, you're such a cynic!" Nancy exclaimed. "It probably comes from spending so much of your professional life dealing with crooks."

"All my clients are innocent until proven guilty," Carson replied with a grin. "But back to your case. What next?"

Nancy rubbed the back of her neck and tried to think. "After the attacks on me and George, it's hard to believe that Jules's death was just a random accident," she said. "So either his killer ran across him by chance—which doesn't explain that note to David—or he knew where Jules was going to be. In that case, we can try to find out who knew, and how."

"Someone at Ellen's open house who overheard Jules's phone call," George said. "Or anyone they might have told. But if they knew the information was important enough to pass along, they were probably part of the scheme already."

Nancy nodded. "Pam said that a lot of the students in the exchange program will be at that picnic this afternoon in Vincennes," she said. "Dad, will you excuse me for a moment? I'm going to call Pam and find out where people are meeting. Having so many suspects in one place should be a real treat."

Following Pam's directions, Nancy and George caught a bus to take them to the park of Vincennes, at the eastern border of Paris. They then walked along a winding path to the edge of a lake. They found several dozen people, including Keith and David, gathered on a grassy point near a footbridge that led to a tiny, tree-covered island.

Pam was standing by herself on the bank of the lake, tossing breadcrumbs to a cluster of eager ducks and geese. She waved. "Isn't this nice?" she said as Nancy and George joined her. "I love picnics, even when it's not summer."

Then she lowered her voice and added, "Don't worry, I'm not forgetting our investigation. What's the program? Is there anybody you want me to grill?"

"Not just now," Nancy said, hiding a smile. She stopped herself from pointing out that at picnics what usually got grilled were hot dogs.

"Nancy?" one of the girls in the group called. As she came over, Nancy tried to recall her name, but couldn't. "I've got a message for you."

Nancy accepted the envelope with her name written in block letters on the front and ripped it open. The note inside was short and to the point.

WATCH OUT, SNOOPER. THERE ARE LOTS MORE TRUCKS IN PARIS.

Chapter Twelve

PAM NOTICED NANCY staring at the threatening note and peered over her shoulder to read it. "Oh!" she exclaimed, shuddering. "How awful! Maria, where did this come from?"

The girl who had brought Nancy the note seemed to be confused. "It was in one of the food bags," she said. "I came across it when I was hunting for the paper napkins. What's wrong?"

"Nothing," Nancy said quickly. There was no point in sharing this latest development with everyone at the picnic.

"That's the same trick David claims somebody used to get that note to him." George said quietly. "Simply leave it where someone's bound to find it and pass it on. What about the handwriting?"

Nancy was already studying the note more closely. The writer had obviously tried to make the block letters as anonymous-looking as possible. No feature stood out, but if she could compare the note to samples of the suspects' handwriting, she might be able to spot something.

Nancy folded the note and put it in her jacket pocket. Ellen would probably have various forms that the students in the exchange program had filled out. She could ask to look through them later, when she got home.

"Did you see who put the note in the food bag?" she asked Maria. "They forgot to sign it."

Maria shook her head. "I found it there, that's all," she said.

"Okay, thanks," Nancy replied. As Maria went back to putting out the supplies for the picnic, Nancy turned to George and Pam and said in an undertone, "Let's separate and talk to as many people as we can. Find out what they did at the end of the party last night, and with whom."

"Why?" Pam demanded. "Did something happen?"

"I'll tell you about it later," Nancy replied. "And ask people about that envelope, too. Somebody may have noticed the person slipping it into the bag."

George and Pam strolled off in different directions. Nancy watched them for a moment, then looked around for Cindy. Would she confirm giving David the note at the open house?

Nancy finally located her on the fringe of a group of picnickers. "I thought it was a little funny, finding an urgent message just sitting next to the telephone like that," Cindy admitted with a frown. "But I figured whoever took the message got distracted and forgot to pass it on. It gave me a real shiver when I heard about Jules. That may have been his last message. Did David meet him the way he was supposed to?"

"I don't think so," Nancy replied. So David's story had been correct, though there was still the possibility that he had written the note himself.

"Were you at that studio party last night?" Nancy added. "There was such a crowd—"

"I dropped in," Cindy said. "But I wasn't feeling well, so I stayed only a few minutes. How late did it go on?"

"I don't know," Nancy replied. "I left around one. Oh—you didn't see anyone put this note in one of the food bags this morning, did you?"

Cindy looked at her, puzzled. "No, why?" she demanded.

"It wasn't signed, so I'm trying to find out who it's from. Oh, well, I'll just keep asking."

Twenty minutes later she began to think she was wasting her time. No one admitted knowing anything about the note, and the information people gave about leaving the party the night before was vague. When Nancy collected Pam and George, they reported the same frustration.

"Listen," Nancy said with sudden decision. "You guys stay here. I want to go home and try to fit some more pieces of the puzzle together."

Pam seemed surprised, but all she said was, "Sure, Nancy. We'll join you there later."

Nancy walked across the park toward the bus stop, her thoughts swirling. What was this case about? Josephine Solo had died in an accident, that was clear. And Jules? The fact that his briefcase had vanished made his death look suspicious. It also formed a link between his death and the life, if not the death, of Solo. The attacks on Nancy that had started after her visit to Censier's gallery made it clear that the attacker knew she was investigating Solo's last months.

Nancy continued mulling over the case on the bus back. She marveled that Paris was a ghost town on a Sunday afternoon. Every store had its steel shutters down. The sidewalks were empty. There were so few cars that Nancy had an impulse to walk down the center of the street. She resisted, in case a Pizza Pow! mobylette should come along and take her out.

Upstairs, Nancy took out all her notes on the case, spread them over the kitchen table, and began shifting them around, hoping for some fresh insight.

Her eye fell on the list she had made of Solo's

appointments. Who on earth was BW? Solo had met with him or her at least twice a week, sometimes more often, during her last months. But there was no one in her address book who fit the initials. Maybe they weren't initials at all, maybe Josephine Solo made a note in her appointment book whenever there was *B*ad *W*eather. Nancy laughed, but made a mental note to check the weather records for Paris during those months.

And what about *CL?* The scrap of paper that Nancy had found in Jules's room linked CL to the other mystery person, G.A. But there was no CL in Solo's address book.

Nancy found her copy of Jules's note and studied it with mounting excitement. CL 381–44961210 . . . She didn't know what to make of the first part, but those eight digits that began with a four could be a Paris phone number. Crossing her fingers, Nancy went over to the telephone and punched in the number.

After two chimed notes, a recorded voice told her that the number she had reached was not in service. Either her idea was wrong, or CL had stopped paying his phone bills. She went back to the kitchen and spread out her notes again.

The list she had copied at Jules's happened to end up dead center. Nancy stared at it longer, with growing puzzlement. Why did her mind insist on seeing the initials CL in yellow, against a blue background? Some mental glitch, or was it something she had seen somewhere recently?

"Of course!" she said aloud. She had walked past it every day! It was the emblem of the Crédit Lyonnais, one of the biggest bank chains in France. One of the branches was just down the street. And the long number next to it had to be an account number. The account of Solo's blackmailer, G.A., for example. . . .

A sudden thought cooled her enthusiasm. Obviously Jules had gotten that list of payments from some sort of financial document of Solo's, such as a bank statement. What if he had jotted down *her* account number at the same time?

Nancy couldn't wait to check on this possibility. She called Ellen. "Do you happen to recall what bank Josephine Solo had her account with?" she asked, when the professor answered.

"Why, yes. I had to deal with them as Jo's executor," Ellen replied. "It was BNP—the Banque Nationale de Paris. Why?"

"Did she have any dealings with Crédit Lyonnais?" Nancy continued.

"Not that I know of," said Ellen. "But yesterday I came across a big manila envelope of miscellaneous financial records that I haven't had time to check out yet."

"Would you mind if I came up and looked through them?" Nancy asked. "I'll be careful not to mislay anything."

The professor hesitated, then said, "No, that's all right. But are you free to come now? I have to go out a little later."

"I'll be right there." Nancy left a note on the door for George saying where she was going, then went upstairs. Ellen opened the door and led her into her back office. Ellen had already found the envelope of financial records and placed it on the desk. Nancy started to sort through the thick stack of papers.

She was a little more than halfway through the stack when she noticed the words Crédit Lyonnais on a flimsy slip of paper. She stopped and read it carefully. It was a duplicate of a deposit slip. Josephine Solo had deposited a check for ten thousand francs—about two thousand dollars—to an account whose number matched that on the slip of paper Nancy had found on Jules's desk. And the name of the account holder was Giuseppina Aria—*G.A.!*

Nancy took a deep breath. Then she sprang up and rushed off to find Ellen. "You remember those payments you discovered?" she demanded. "Well, I've just found out who they were made to."

She showed Ellen the deposit slip and explained what she thought it meant.

"Aria," Ellen said thoughtfully. "I don't know anybody by that name in Jo's circle of friends."

"A blackmailer?" Nancy said.

"You know," Ellen said thoughtfully, "in French, a blackmailer is called a *maître-chanteur*, or singing-master, because he makes his victims 'sing.' I wonder if this mysterious Aria chose the name for that reason, as a sort of sick joke. And now that I think of it, after Jo's death, I found a key ring on her dresser marked Aria. But why would she have her blackmailer's keys?"

"I don't know," Nancy replied. "But could I borrow them? They might be important."

While Ellen went off in search of the key ring, Nancy studied the deposit slip. How could she manage to track down Aria? Impossible to ask the bank on a Sunday, and even on Monday, the chances weren't good that they would give her any information about their account holder.

The rubber stamp indicated that the branch was in Paris near Montmartre. Why not try the obvious approach first? When Ellen returned, Nancy asked, "Do you have a Paris phone book?"

The professor smiled. "Phone books are out of date. Here in France, there's a computerized system called Minitel." She led Nancy over to what looked like a miniature computer terminal and pushed a few buttons. The screen lit up.

"Just type the name of the person you want to get the number of, and the address, if you know it," Ellen explained.

Nancy typed ARIA, then PARIS, and hit the Send button. After a short pause, three names and addresses appeared on the screen. The first was a film company. The second was someone named Philippe Aria. And the third was—*G. Aria!*

Chapter Thirteen

NANCY BLINKED, then looked again at the entry on the Minitel screen. It was still there, in white on black: ARIA G., 37, R POULBOT, 75018 PARIS, 1 43 48 13 12.

"Hooray!" Nancy shouted. Then she grabbed a pen and scratch pad and copied the information, just in case she pushed the wrong key and it somehow vanished forever from the screen.

Ellen, alerted by Nancy's shout, came back. Nancy showed her the entry.

"This is exciting," Ellen said. "Imagine if I could recover some of Jo's money for my university's museum."

Nancy reached for the telephone, took a deep breath, and dialed Aria's number. There was a series of rapid clicks, then it started to ring. Nancy let it ring fifteen times before hanging up.

"No one home," she reported. "But at least the phone is connected. As soon as George gets back, we can pay a visit to rue Poulbot. Will you come with us?"

Ellen shook her head. "I wish I could, but I have an engagement I can't break. You will keep me informed, though, won't you?"

"Sure," Nancy promised. She recalled the threatening note she had received at the picnic. "Oh—do you have anything in the handwriting of the students in the program that I could look at?"

"Why?" Ellen asked.

Nancy showed her the note and explained how she had received it. "It had to be somebody at the picnic who sent it," she concluded.

"Hmmm—yes, I think I have something that will help," the professor said. She opened the file drawer in her desk, pulled out a thick folder, and began leafing through it.

"All the students wrote essays about why they wanted to come to Paris," she said. "I don't think they'd mind my letting you see them."

Together they leafed through the stack of handwritten essays, pausing now and then to study the note again. Finally Ellen shook her head. "A professional graphologist might be able to say who wrote that note," she said. "But I certainly can't."

"I can't, either," Nancy confessed. "But it had

to be someone at the picnic, and everyone there was from your program."

"But why would one of our students want to keep you from investigating Jules's death?" Ellen asked. "You don't really think that Jules was killed by one of our group, do you?"

"I don't know what to think," Nancy admitted. "I've been going on the theory that somebody in the program is in cahoots with G.A. and is trying to scare us off the case. But that doesn't mean he or she is a murderer."

The doorbell rang. Ellen went to answer it. "Come in, girls," she said. "Nancy's made an amazing discovery."

Nancy felt a little superstitious shiver at the professor's choice of words. Wasn't that what Jules had said, not long before he died? It seemed likely now that his amazing discovery was about Giuseppina Aria.

"Nancy, what is it?" George demanded, rushing into the room with Pam. "What did you find out?"

Nancy showed them the Minitel screen and explained how she had tracked down G.A. "Who's up for a visit to the rue Poulbot?" she concluded.

"I am," George and Pam both said instantly.

Ellen was studying her Paris guide. "I've located the street," she reported. "It's in Montmartre, not far from the place du Tertre."

Nancy was startled. "Really? That's where the

gallery of that guy Leduc is. I wonder if there's a connection."

"Let's find out," George said.

"Good luck," Ellen said as the three girls headed for the door. "Be careful."

Fifteen minutes later their taxi dropped them at the mouth of the rue Poulbot. It was a narrow street, paved with cobblestones, that sloped steeply downhill, then curved to the left. The houses along it were low for Paris houses, only two and three stories high.

Nancy led the way to number 37, which was on the downhill side of the street. The outer door was locked, of course. Next to it were three buzzers. One was labeled Mikolajczak, and a second, Simoneau. The third had no name on it.

"Aria?" Nancy said to her friends. "Let's try."

She pressed the buzzer and waited. There was no response. She pressed it again. Nothing.

"Why don't we try the neighbors?" George suggested. "At least we can ask them some questions about Aria."

No one responded to the other buzzers either. Frustrated, Nancy glanced at her watch and said, "Let's get a snack and come back in twenty minutes. Maybe someone will be home by then."

The place du Tertre was just up the hill. Nancy hardly recognized it. On a sunny Sunday afternoon, it seethed with people. The crowd was so thick that it was impossible to take more than two or three steps without stopping.

The center of the square was divided among half a dozen different cafés and restaurants, each with its own distinctive tables and chairs. Standing on tiptoe to see over the crowd, Nancy spotted a family just getting up from a table with a yellow and green cloth.

"Over there," she muttered to George and Pam. She dodged a woman with a baby in a stroller, edged around the easel of a sidewalk portrait artist, and wiggled through the narrow aisle to the vacant table.

"Whew!" George said, after they ordered sandwiches and lemonades. "Who *are* all these people, and what are they doing here?"

Pam smiled. "They're tourists, just like us," she said. "And they've come to see Montmartre because they've heard about it all their lives. Toulouse-Lautrec, the Moulin Rouge, all that. But once they get here, what they mostly see is other tourists."

When the sandwiches arrived, Nancy realized how hungry she was. She hadn't eaten since brunch. Was that the reason her brain felt sluggish? She was sure that they were practically on the point of solving the case, yet she couldn't see her way out.

"This is really the pits," George said, when the three had finished their sandwiches. "The solution is probably right over there in that apartment, and all that stands in our way is a couple of locked doors. Too bad we don't have keys for them."

Nancy slapped herself on the forehead and exclaimed, *"We do!"* She was vaguely aware of people at nearby tables turning to look at her. With an effort, she took a deep breath and continued in a calmer voice.

"I'm a hopeless idiot," she told Pam and George. "Ellen found a ring of keys labeled Aria among Josephine Solo's belongings. I borrowed them from her, and then forgot all about them. They're right here in my pocket."

George stared at her for a moment, then pushed her chair back. "What are we waiting for?" she demanded, dropping some money on the table. "Let's roll."

It seemed to Nancy that the crowd had thickened until it was on the point of setting like cement. Muttering *"Pardon"* and *"Excusez-moi,"* she forced her way through to the edge of the square, with George and Pam close behind, then walked faster to the corner of rue Poulbot. At Number 37, she rang Aria's bell again, just to be safe, then tried the larger of the two keys. It worked.

"Which floor?" George whispered, once they were inside.

"It was the top buzzer," Nancy pointed out. "Let's try the top floor, then work our way down if we have to."

The stairs creaked loudly. At every step, Nancy imagined someone appearing suddenly and demanding to know what they were doing.

At the head of the stairs was a single door. A card taped to it said Aria. Nancy knocked on the door and waited a few seconds, but there was no sound of movement inside. She used the second key, pushed the door open—and let out a gasp.

The room was big, at least twenty feet by thirty, with high ceilings. Directly across from the door was a wall that was practically all windows. All of Paris was laid out below, as if they were peering down from a low-flying plane.

Nancy tore her attention away from the panorama and took in the room itself. It was furnished as a painter's studio, with three easels and a big, solid worktable in the center, a couple of comfortable chairs, and, in one corner, a compact kitchenette unit.

Was this the headquarters of a blackmailer?

While George and Pam prowled around the room, Nancy went over to one of the easels and examined the painting it held. Only half finished, it was an abstract in blues and grays that reminded Nancy of a stormy day at sea. She liked it, and she thought she recognized the style.

With growing excitement, she looked around the studio. Just behind the door, a bright yellow rain suit was hanging on a coatrack. On the floor under it was a pair of lobsterman's rubber boots.

"Pam! George!" Nancy shouted, suddenly sure. Alarmed, the other two hurried over to her.

"Giuseppina Aria," Nancy said. "What's Giuseppina? The Italian form of the name, Josephine. And what's an aria? An operatic *solo.* Don't you see? We had it all wrong. Giuseppina Aria wasn't blackmailing Josephine Solo. Giuseppina Aria *was* Josephine Solo!"

Chapter Fourteen

GEORGE'S JAW DROPPED in astonishment. "You mean Solo was leading a double life?" she demanded. "Why?"

"And how?" added Pam, who was just as amazed.

"I don't know," Nancy admitted. "But lots of people, at some point in their lives, get the feeling that they'd like to start over with a clean slate. Maybe that was how Solo felt."

Pam was unconvinced. "I don't get it. She was famous, her paintings were selling for a lot of money, she could do whatever she wanted. Why start over, if you've got it all?"

Good question, Nancy thought. What had led Josephine Solo, at the height of her career, to want to become someone else? Then her eye fell on the uncompleted painting. It was as if Solo were speaking to her directly.

"Her work," Nancy said. "Look at the painting on the easel. It's in her earlier style, not the one that made her famous. Maybe she never really liked hyperrealism, even though she was so good at it. We'll have to ask Ellen. She may have some insights into Solo's frame of mind."

George gestured toward a long wooden rack near the door. Its two shelves were jammed with stacked canvases. "Whatever the reason, she certainly put a lot of effort into her new life," she said. "There must be thirty or forty paintings in that rack."

Pam let out a whistle. "Do you have any idea how much just *one* painting by Solo sells for these days?" she demanded. "We're looking at millions of dollars!"

"Maybe," Nancy said, walking over to the rack. She pulled out one of the canvases. As she expected, it, too, was an abstract, this time in dark, ominous shades. It was not signed or dated.

"Or maybe not," she continued. "A Solo sells for a lot, sure. But these aren't Solos, they're Arias. And in any case, under Solo's will they all go to Ellen's university. That should be a nice surprise for the people there."

George scratched her head and said, "I'm still in the dark. Okay, Solo wanted to go back to painting the way she used to paint. Why didn't she just do it, then? Lots of famous painters move from one style to another, don't they? Look at Picasso—I don't even remember how many different styles he worked in."

"I don't know," Nancy replied. "We may have to wait for Ellen's biography of Solo to find out. But maybe she wanted people to look at her new work without always thinking that it was by Josephine Solo."

"What do you suppose she was planning to do?" Pam wondered. "Just vanish?"

Nancy tried to imagine herself in Solo's shoes. "If I were she, I would have changed my bank account and gotten the new studio. Then, when the time came, I would have told everybody I knew that I'd decided to leave Paris, and I'd move to New Zealand or Montana or Nepal—some place fairly remote. Then I'd find new hangouts. In a town the size of Paris, that wouldn't be hard. And if I happened to run into somebody I knew, I'd say I was just passing through. It would probably work. Remember, we're not talking about hiding out from the police. Nobody would be actively trying to find her. She just hadn't gotten around to disappearing before she was run over by a truck."

"To think that this place has been sitting here gathering dust ever since she died," Pam said. "It's spooky. Why didn't anybody find out about it, like the phone company or the landlord?"

"I've been wondering about that, too," Nancy said, her eyes sweeping the studio. In the corner near the door was a small pile of envelopes. She picked them up. There were half a dozen from Crédit Lyonnais, Aria's bank. On one, the flap was unglued. Nancy opened it. Inside was a one-page bank statement.

"So that's it," Nancy said, after scanning the statement. "Solo, as Aria, must have owned this studio. And she arranged for her bank to pay the carrying charges and the utilities automatically, every month. As long as there was enough money in the account to cover the bills, no one would have any reason to suspect anything."

After a pause, she added, "No one—except Jules."

"You think this was his amazing discovery?" George asked.

"I doubt if he knew about this studio," Nancy replied. "But we know he found out about Aria's bank account, and he may have figured out that Aria was Solo. He knew a lot more about Solo's life than we did, after all. He'd been studying her daily activities, her moods, everything. Her moods—why were we so blind? Gail, one of the people who knew Solo best, told us that she'd never seen her happier. But someone who's being bled dry by a blackmailer doesn't go around being happy. We should have known that we were on the wrong track."

"We have to tell Ellen about this right away," George said. "She's going to be shocked out of her mind. Let's go find a telephone."

"There's one here somewhere," Nancy reminded her. "And as of this morning, it was working."

"I don't see it," Pam said. "Do you suppose it's in the closet?" She went over to a narrow door and pulled it open.

"Oh, look!" she exclaimed. "It's not a closet, it's a bedroom. And there's the phone."

Nancy and George followed Pam into the small room. The only furnishings were a narrow bed, a dresser, and a wicker chair next to the window. The telephone was on the floor next to the bed.

Nancy was about to dial Ellen's number when George raised her head, suddenly alert. Nancy gave her an inquiring glance. George put her finger to her lips, then pointed toward the half-open door to the studio. Nancy heard it, too—the faint sound of cautious footsteps. Someone was out there!

"We'd better let the professor know about this," Nancy said in a normal tone of voice as she tiptoed toward the door. She gestured for George and Pam to follow her.

"What is it?" Pam demanded, alarmed. "Is there someone—"

From the studio, Nancy heard a sudden rush of footsteps. She dashed through the doorway, but already the studio was empty. The front door stood ajar. The intruder had escaped.

Pam was nearest to the door. She ran out onto the landing. Nancy and George were close behind her. A black-clad figure was vaulting down the stairs, three at a time. Nancy had just enough time to glimpse a black leather wristband. A moment later, the downstairs door slammed shut.

Nancy ran down the stairs and out the door, but the narrow, dead-end street was empty. At the corner where it joined a major street, a steady stream of tourists flowed past.

"No point in chasing him," Nancy said to Pam and George, who had joined her. "There are so many people on the street that we'd never manage to find him."

Pam grabbed Nancy's arm. "But, Nancy—that was Keith!" she gasped. "I'm sure it was! What was he doing here? Why did he run away?"

Nancy met George's eyes. A lot of questions had just been answered.

"He must have followed us here," Nancy replied. She turned to re-enter the building, then paused and added, "I just realized something else. The person who attacked me in the courtyard last night was wearing a leather wristband."

"Keith attacked you?" Pam whispered. "Oh, no. There must be a mistake. He'd never—"

"I'm sorry, Pam," Nancy said. "But I'm wondering if Keith is really the person you think he is. Did you ever get the feeling that he's spent a lot of time in Paris before this semester? He seems to know a lot of people and a lot about the town for someone who arrived in September."

"I did wonder about it," Pam admitted. "But so what if he's been here before?"

"I don't know," Nancy said. "I'm moving pieces of the puzzle around, hoping that some will fit together. Keith's a painter, and he knows Paris. What if he spent time here before and got to know Josephine Solo? He knows a lot about her work and has strong opinions about it, that's for sure. I noticed that at the open house."

George eyed Nancy closely. "Do you mean that Keith is our bad guy?"

Nancy hesitated. "Well, it's starting to look that way," she said finally. "Pam, have you ever seen Keith wear a dark green jumpsuit?"

Pam gave her a nervous look. "He paints in something like that," she replied. "Why?"

"The guy who tried to run us down the other day was wearing one," George explained.

"Oh, no," Pam said, with a hint of a sob. "I know Keith better than that. I'm sure he'd never hurt anybody on purpose. If it was he, maybe he was just trying to scare you."

"If so, he succeeded," Nancy said.

"We should go upstairs and call Ellen, right now," Pam said. "She has to know about this. And what about calling the police?"

"We should definitely call Ellen," Nancy said.

"As for the police, I think we need some advice about how to deal with them. It's all pretty fuzzy, what we have to tell them. Maybe my dad will have some ideas about how to handle the situation."

Nancy returned to the bedroom and dialed Ellen's number. George and Pam followed her in. After four rings the answering machine picked up. Nancy left a message explaining where they were and what they had found. As she was finishing, she heard an odd click. The line went dead.

"That's funny," she said, turning to George and Pam. "I wonder what—"

Suddenly the bedroom door slammed shut. Nancy rushed over and twisted the knob, but it did no good. Someone had locked them in!

Chapter Fifteen

THE INSTANT Pam realized that someone had locked them in, she rushed over to the door and started pounding on it with her fists.

"Let us out of here," she shouted, her voice close to hysterical. "Please, let us out!"

Nancy took Pam by the shoulders and turned her away from the door. "Save your energy," she advised. "You'll need it later."

Meanwhile, George had rushed over to the window and tugged at it. It didn't budge.

"What's the story?" Nancy asked when her friend had turned back.

"No good," George reported, shaking her head. "It's painted shut. And the building's on a steep slope, so we're what amounts to five or six floors high. No fire escapes, either. We'll just have to wait for someone to let us out."

"Why did Keith lock us in?" Pam demanded. "I'll never forgive him for this. I've always *hated* being shut up, and he knows it!"

Nancy realized that, stripped of its emotional overtones, Pam's question was a good one. Why *had* Keith—if it was Keith—locked them in? What did he hope to accomplish?

"Nancy," George said in a low voice, "I hear voices in the other room."

Nancy went to the door and pressed her ear against it. George was right, there were voices. Two of them. One voice had the timbre of Keith's, but the other was unfamiliar. Nancy couldn't make out any words, but after a moment she heard something bump on the floor, followed by the sound of footsteps that seemed to leave the studio. She remained at the door, barely breathing. After several minutes of silence the footsteps returned, followed by more bumping noises and another departure. A few minutes later, the pattern repeated itself a third time.

"What is it? What's happening out there?" Pam demanded.

"I'm not sure," Nancy responded grimly. "But I can guess. You're the one who pointed out that the paintings out there are worth millions. Well, it looks as if a couple of people—Keith is probably one of them—have decided to take those millions for themselves. I think they're carrying the canvases away at this very moment."

Nancy scrutinized the door, but it was obviously too solid to break down. The lock was old fashioned, but it, too, was solid. Was there something she could use to try to pick it? She began to prowl around the room for anything to use as a tool. After a few minutes she realized that her search was pointless. The closest she came to something useful was an ordinary nail file, and there was no way to bend that into an effective lockpick.

"Nancy, come listen," George whispered urgently. "They're arguing."

Nancy joined George at the door and listened. It did sound like an argument, though only Keith's voice was raised, and he was speaking in French.

No, not speaking—shouting. *"Je ne te laisserai pas passer ça!"* he said. "I won't let you get away with that!"

There was the sickening sound of a blow, then the thump of a body hitting the floor. A few moments later the outer door slammed.

"What happened?" Pam demanded.

"I think Keith and his partner had a falling out," Nancy reported.

"What were they arguing about?" George asked. "How to split up the loot?"

"Maybe," Nancy said thoughtfully. "But I don't think so. I heard Keith say something about a dirty trick and not going along with it."

"He isn't all bad, then," Pam said. "Maybe he'll let us out of here."

"I doubt if he's in any shape to," Nancy replied, remembering the sound of the falling body.

"There's something I don't understand," George said. "How do the crooks expect to get away with those paintings? Once we tell the authorities about finding the paintings here, it's all over for them. They'll never be able to sell them. Didn't they think of that?"

Nancy sniffed the air, then sniffed again, before saying grimly, "I'm afraid they did. I smell smoke. And we're locked in. Unless we find a way out fast, I don't think we're going to be telling the authorities anything!"

"Oh, no!" Pam exclaimed. Her face turned white. "Nancy, George, what are we going to do?"

"We'll just have to think of something," Nancy replied. She rattled the door handle, then tugged at it. There was no give at all. When she backed off a couple of steps and slammed into the center of the door, all she got was a sore shoulder.

The smell of smoke was stronger now. Nancy could see little gray wisps drifting in through the gap at the bottom of the door.

"I hate being locked in," Pam said, her voice shrill. "I *hate* it!"

"What if we shout for help?" George asked.

"It's worth trying," Nancy replied, and then, in a voice too low for Pam to hear, added, "but I doubt if anyone will get here in time."

George nodded and went over to the window. Wrapping her leather jacket around her fist, she smashed one of the panes, then leaned out and began shouting, *"Au feu! Au feu!"*

Nancy studied the bottom of the door. The smoke was thicker and darker now. She recalled a trick she had read about. Could it possibly work?

Moving quickly, she picked up the nail file and tore a sheet of paper from a sketchpad. After getting down on one knee, she slid the paper under the door, carefully positioning it under the door handle. Then she bent closer to the old-fashioned lock, peered through the keyhole, and gave a loud sigh of relief. The key was still there. She had been counting on that.

As carefully as a surgeon performing an operation, Nancy inserted the nail file into the keyhole and felt for the rounded end of the key's shaft. Twice the point of the file slipped past the key. Nancy stopped and wiped her palms on her shirt sleeves, then tried again. This time, she felt resistance when she moved the file. She pressed a little harder, but nothing happened. Was the key stuck in the lock? If so, there was no hope.

Taking a deep breath, Nancy pushed still harder. Suddenly the key slipped out of the lock and clattered to the floor. Had it landed on the sheet of paper or bounced off? She slowly pulled the edge of the paper toward her. To her relief, she felt the weight of the key on it. Now she had to slide the paper back under the door without knocking the key off.

"Nancy, hurry!" Pam called. Then she broke into a fit of coughing.

Nancy shut her mind to Pam and George, to the smoke in the air, to everything except the weight of the key on the sheet of paper. She inched the paper toward herself, then stopped when she felt the key bump against the bottom edge of the door. Was there room for it to clear? She lay down on her stomach and peered under the door. The floor was irregular, making the gap a little larger to the left. She slid the paper in that direction, then pulled it toward her again.

"Yes!" she shouted as the tip of the key appeared under the door. She grabbed it and put it in the lock and turned it. Before opening the door, she pressed her palm to the center panel. It felt a little warm, but not hot. "Come on, you two, let's get out of here," she yelled to George and Pam.

The upper half of the big studio was dark with smoke. Nancy knelt and quickly scanned the room. The shelves that had held Solo's paintings were empty now. Under them, a pile of rags smoldered. So far, the fire had been contained to the rags, but suddenly, as Nancy watched, a tongue of flame shot up and began to lick the charred upright that supported the shelves.

"Water, quick!" Nancy shouted. George ran to the kitchenette and started filling pans at the sink. Nancy and Pam ran back and forth pouring water over the burning rags. The smoke turned white. At last the flames vanished.

"Keith!" Pam shouted.

Nancy turned. Pam was rushing toward the door, where a person dressed in black lay face-down on the floor. Nancy hurried to join her. Keith had a nasty-looking bump on the left side of his head, just above the ear. Nancy felt the pulse in his neck. It was strong and steady.

"He'll be all right, I think," she told Pam. "Let's drag him out onto the stairway. Fresh air will help."

She took one arm, and Pam and George the other. As they tugged Keith through the doorway, he stirred and muttered something over and over. Nancy leaned closer. It sounded like "Jean-Luc."

"Censier! Of course!" Nancy exclaimed. She turned to George and Pam. The words came in a rush. "Who else would be in a position to sell those paintings? Jean-Luc Censier—Solo's dealer for years. And with Keith out of the way, he won't have to split the profits."

Nancy could hear the two-toned horn of a fire

engine coming closer. Someone must have heard George's shouts and sounded the alarm.

"What now?" George demanded. "If the fire fighters find us in an apartment that isn't ours, we'll be answering questions for the next day and a half!"

"You're right," Nancy said quickly. "We can't give Censier time to get all those paintings to a safe hiding place. Let's get out of here."

"And leave Keith here?" Pam protested. "We can't do that!"

The fire engine was practically outside the building now.

"Fine," Nancy said. "You stay with him, then. And as soon as you can, call Professor Mathieson and my father and tell them what's going on. Tell them to alert the police. George and I are going to track down Censier to recover the stolen paintings."

Darkness was falling as Nancy and George rushed from the building. The fire engine had just come to a halt across the mouth of the narrow street. Four fire fighters, in rubber coats and steel helmets, all pulling a hose, ran past the two girls and into the building. A crowd started to gather.

Once past the fire engine, Nancy spotted a taxi stand. "Come on."

The first few blocks seemed to take forever. Their cab got stuck behind a vehicle painted to resemble an old-time steam train. The dozens of tourists riding in it were obviously having a fine time taking photos of Montmartre, but Nancy was ready to start biting her nails.

Finally the vehicle made a left turn, and Nancy had to grab the edge of her seat, as the taxi driver swerved past it, accelerating to make up for the time he'd lost.

The taxi stopped on the rue Bonaparte, and Nancy and George got out. Steel shutters were drawn across the windows and door of the Galerie Censier. Nancy shaded her eyes and peered through one of the cracks. Was that a light in the back room?

"Let's take a look around," Nancy said. "Maybe there's another way in."

They started to circle the block. On the side street, George pointed to a narrow lane. An ornate metal gate blocked the entrance, but Nancy managed to snake an arm through and press the button that released the lock. She hurried down the lane, with George close behind. Fifty feet in, the lane bent to the right and became a courtyard. A van was backed up to one of the buildings, evidently the back of the gallery. Nancy and George approached the van, and Nancy peered in through the rear door. By the dim light of a street lamp, she could make out a half dozen paintings inside.

"George, this is it!" she said exultantly. "We've—"

"Nancy, look out!" George shouted.

Nancy whirled around. From the rear door of the gallery, Jean-Luc Censier was charging toward her, a crowbar in his right hand raised high, ready to strike a deadly blow.

Chapter Sixteen

As THE ENRAGED gallery owner ran at her, Nancy threw herself sideways and to the ground. Censier slammed the crowbar against the roof of the van with a terrible *clang,* then let out a cry of pain and grabbed his hand. The crowbar clattered to the pavement.

Nancy rose and dove at Censier, wrapping her arms around his knees. Off balance, he staggered and fell backward, landing heavily. He groaned as his head banged against a cobblestone.

"Quick, George," Nancy shouted, jumping up and standing over the dazed man. "Go inside and find something we can use to tie him up."

As George vanished through the open door, Nancy heard running footsteps in the lane. The cavalry to the rescue? Or another enemy to be faced? She quickly bent down and picked up the crowbar, then stood with her feet apart and her knees slightly bent, ready for action. Her heartbeat sounded very loud in her ears.

Someone dressed all in black appeared at the entrance to the courtyard. He paused for an instant, swaying slightly, then broke into a run in Nancy's direction. It was Keith. He must have overpowered Pam and made his escape, before the fire fighters found him. Now he had come to claim his share of a fortune in stolen paintings, and only Nancy and George stood in his way.

Nancy tightened her grip on the crowbar, wondering if she could bring herself to use it as a weapon. Keith had already suffered one serious blow that day. A second one, so soon afterward, might do permanent damage.

Nancy made a lightning decision and dropped the crowbar. She would have to rely on her reflexes, knowledge of judo, and Keith's weakened state to help overcome him.

Keith was halfway across the courtyard when he shouted, "Nancy, behind you!" She scowled and went deeper into her fighting stance. Did he really think she would fall for that old gag? Then, out of the corner of her eye, she noticed movement. She turned, just as Censier lurched to his feet and rushed to grab the crowbar again.

Before Nancy had time to react, Keith launched himself in a flying tackle—at Censier. Once more the crowbar whistled through the air, and once more it missed its target. The gallery owner crashed to the ground, with Keith on top of him. Censier aimed a blow at Keith's jaw. Keith slumped like a rag doll. Censier pushed him aside and began to scramble to his feet again.

In a flash Nancy was on him. She grabbed his left wrist and twisted his arm into a hammerlock, then used her knee in the small of his back to force him, facedown, to the pavement. George came running out of the gallery with a spool of picture wire and a pair of pliers. Moments later, Censier was bound and helpless, and Keith was sitting up, rubbing his jaw.

Pam came running up and took Nancy's arm. "We got here as fast as we could," she panted. "Keith promised to tell the whole story to the police. I called your dad and he's contacting the cops. They should be on their way here, with David. He was really worried about us."

"I was pretty worried myself," Nancy said dryly.

The police took Keith and Censier under guard to a nearby hospital for examination. Two officers stayed behind to oversee the transfer of the paintings to a bank vault for safekeeping. Nancy and the others returned to Ellen's apartment.

"I think I've grasped the broad outlines of what's been going on," Carson Drew said. "But I'm pretty fuzzy on the details. How did Keith and Censier know those paintings existed?"

"They didn't, Dad," Nancy replied. "It was a guess on their part. But as Solo's agent, Censier knew how dissatisfied she'd been with the work she was doing. And when she stopped doing it, he guessed she was doing something else. Maybe she let something slip during the argument they had."

"And Keith?" David asked. "Where did he come into it?"

Nancy said, "That's an interesting story. George and I figured that he knew too much about Paris for this to be his first stay. And he's an art student. It seemed possible that his path had crossed Solo's at some point."

"Did it ever!" Pam interjected. "He told me all about it in the cab on our way to the gallery. Solo took him under her wing. She really liked his work and thought he had a lot of talent. She used to call him her Boy Wonder."

"Huh!" Nancy said. "So that's who the mysterious BW in her datebook was! Sorry, Pam, go on."

"Solo's death really shook him up," Pam continued. "He left Paris and went back to the States. But then he started wondering about some of the things she had said about making a clean break with her old life. He wondered what she had meant. He was sure that she had done many more paintings than had surfaced. Where were the rest?"

Nancy took up the story. "So Keith came back

to Paris as part of the exchange program. I suspect part of the reason he joined the program was that he knew about Ellen's research into Solo's life."

"Hmmph! The nerve," Ellen muttered.

"Once here, he got in touch with Censier," Nancy continued. "They made a deal to find the missing paintings and share the profits."

"How could they have hoped to sell them?" Carson asked. "As I understand it, Solo left her entire estate in trust to Ellen. Once those paintings surfaced, title would automatically pass to Ellen."

"They thought of that," Pam told him. "Censier was planning to say, and back it up with phony documents, that when Solo decided to turn to hyperrealism, she sold him all the paintings she had around in her old abstract style. They were going to be sold as old Solos, not new Arias."

Nancy took up the story, as she had pieced it together from Pam's statements on the way over. "Part of Keith's job was to keep a close eye on Jules and try to take advantage of any discoveries he made," she said. "So he overheard Ellen talking to Jules over the phone during Ellen's party."

"He must have heard me asking Jules what his amazing discovery was," Ellen said.

Pam broke in. "But Keith swears he never thought anybody would get hurt."

"Except Jules," David pointed out.

Pam turned to face her twin brother. "All Keith meant to do was snatch Jules's briefcase," she declared. "I know that wasn't right, but it's not the same as murder. It wasn't totally his fault that Jules stumbled into the street and was hit by a truck."

"That's for the courts to decide," George interjected. "And one woman said she thought Jules was knocked into the path of the truck. Also, he tried to set David up as the fall guy simply because he didn't like him. But in any case, whatever he found in the briefcase convinced Keith that he was on the right track. But we were on the track, too, and on *his* track. He tried to scare us off with the mobylette, the attacks on Nancy, and the note, but when that didn't work, he decided to use us instead."

"He could have killed me on the steps at Montmartre. That was a bit much for a scare tactic," Nancy said. "And then today, he must have followed us to Montmartre again. Once he was sure that we'd located Solo's studio, he telephoned Censier, who came right over with a van. You know the rest."

"Not quite," Ellen said. "Why did Censier knock Keith out and try to set the studio on fire?"

"He had to silence us," Nancy explained. "Otherwise, his scheme for selling the paintings as Solo's early work couldn't possibly work. And when Keith objected, he decided he had to silence him, too. Who knows? Maybe he meant to get rid of Keith all along."

"A real sweetheart," David growled. "I hope they put him away for a long time."

Carson said, "Arson, theft, assault, attempted murder . . . I imagine they will, thanks to all of you."

"How are you going to spend the rest of your visit to Paris, girls?" asked Ellen. "After everything you've been through, I'm afraid that mere sightseeing will seem terribly dull."

George met Nancy's eyes and started to laugh. "Who could possibly find Paris dull?" she demanded. "And anyway, we've had enough excitement for a while."

Nancy added, with a twinkle in her eye, "Just don't expect us to spend much time visiting art galleries. They're too dangerous!"

"Well, since you mention galleries," Ellen said, "this is a good time to announce that you and your father and George, and Pam and David, will all be guests of honor when the Solo/Aria wing of my university's art museum is dedicated. I know that poor, dear Jo would have been proud to have you there."

Nancy's next case:

Bess has gotten a real surprise for Christmas: two crisp new twenties that turn out to be fake. Her aunt, who works at *River Heights* magazine, unwittingly passed them along, and Nancy's out to trace the funny money to its source. But there's one very big distraction: suspect Stuart Teal. He has looks to die for . . . and clearly has designs on Nancy. Stuart may want to corner the market on Nancy's affections, but she can't afford to take the chance . . . especially when another top suspect is found dead. Drawn into a world where greed rules and life isn't worth a plug nickel, Nancy has no choice but to keep her eye on the bottom line: She's searching for a counterfeiter who fits the bill of a murderer . . . in *Counterfeit Christmas,* Case #102 in The Nancy Drew Files™.